"It's ha_____
he acknowledged quietly. "I think we
can admit that without hurting each
other's feelings."

Kara looked at him sharply. "Matthew, the case
has me on edge. Not you."

He stiffened and she could almost feel him
physically shutting her out, slamming the door
on any fledgling attempt at civility, and she was
alternately relieved and horrified. Shame. That's
the feeling that was crushing her.

She was ashamed for not having the courage to
tell him that he had a daughter.

Dear Reader,

Sometimes a story comes out of nowhere and the characters grab you by the throat, demanding that you put words to paper. That's what happened with this book. Kara Thistle and Matthew Beauchamp materialized in my mind and wouldn't let go. Theirs is a dark story, but the light of their love ultimately illuminates the path to happiness and joy.

This is my first Silhouette Romantic Suspense novel, and I'm proud of the way it turned out, even if the writing of it was incredibly difficult. I shudder at the places I took my characters, but their strength helped me as well as them as they raced to save a child from a killer.

I hope you enjoy this roller coaster of a read as much as I enjoyed writing it. Hearing from readers is one of my greatest joys (aside from really good chocolate), so don't be shy. Feel free to drop me a line at my Web site, www.kimberlyvanmeter.com, or through snail mail, P.O. Box 2210, Oakdale, CA 95361.

Happy reading,

Kimberly Van Meter

KIMBERLY VAN METER

To Catch a Killer

ROMANTIC
SUSPENSE

 SILHOUETTE BOOKS

ISBN-13: 978-0-373-27692-9

Recycling programs
for this product may
not exist in your area.

TO CATCH A KILLER

Books by Kimberly Van Meter

KIMBERLY VAN METER

wrote her first book at sixteen and finally achieved publication in December 2006. She writes for Harlequin Superromance and Silhouette Romantic Suspense.

She and her husband of seventeen years have three children, three cats and always a houseful of friends, family and fun.

Special thanks go to Lieutenant Vernon Gladney for putting a gun in my hands. He said I couldn't write about an FBI agent without knowing what it feels like to shoot the guns they use every day. He was right. Knowledge is power. And guns…are still scary.

To Sally Grigg, the mistress of the Howard Creek Ranch in Westport, California. Thank you for sharing your knowledge of local flora and fauna and your delicious cooking. I'm still pining for more of your fresh mint tea and homemade biscuits.

To "that guy" in Shelter Cove who filled me in on the "Emerald Triangle" of the northern California coast. Your candid comments were priceless.

Lastly, to John. My traveling partner, friend, husband and lover. Every day you help remind me why love is worth fighting for. Thank you.

Chapter 1

The morning broke gray and dismal. Cloud cover drifted, creeping among the trees of Wolf's Tooth ravine, overgrown with hundred-year-old cedars and western red hemlock. It was a place Matthew Beauchamp would normally enjoy hiking to, but today was no ordinary day.

A freelance photographer taking photos of the area had stumbled upon the body of a little girl. Now, looking down at the body, Matthew thought he had not come across a more heart-rending scene in his entire law enforcement career. Having grown up in the sleepy town of Lantern Cove, Matthew, as chief of police, was more accustomed to crimes of opportunity: petty theft, vandalism, the usual pot smokers and growers. Nothing like this.

Mud spattered her short-sleeve "Princess" shirt and pink sweatpants; she was missing a shoe. Her small toes had the remnants of pink polish and her flaxen hair was matted with dirt and underbrush. Someone had tossed this child away as if she were garbage.

"Feds are on their way. Should be here anytime," Sgt. Oren Lawrence said, coming to stand next to Matthew. Wiping his ruddy nose with the back of his glove, he sucked back the rest of the snot before continuing, "You thinking what I'm thinking?"

Cold seeping into his bones, Matthew nodded. "It's that Linney girl. Went missing a week ago in San Francisco."

"Far from home."

"Yeah," Matthew said grimly. "But only someone who's familiar with this area would've known about Wolf's Tooth. It's not like this place is popular with tourists. It's hard to get to and you risk a broken ankle coming down that ridge." He shook his head.

"How about the shutterbug who found her?" Oren speculated but Matthew shook his head.

"At this point he seems clean. Looked ready to puke. I don't blame him. Coming across a body like this might make any normal person lose his lunch. But I've got Dinky looking into his alibi."

The sound of cars pulling off the shoulder above them drew their attention and Oren grimaced. "Feds." Then he clapped Matthew on the shoulder before returning to the team who were canvassing the area. "Remember to play nice," he said.

Matthew looked up as two agents appeared over the ridge, a man and a woman, and he waved them down.

At first there was nothing extraordinary about the two. They had the look of federal agents, complete with austere coats, serious expressions and an air of arrogance that seemed to come with being affiliated with a government agency. But as they traversed the dangerous, uneven terrain, and walked toward him, Matthew sucked in a sharp breath as recognition hit him in a flash, knocking the wind out of him. He hadn't seen her in almost ten years but he'd recognize that face anywhere.

Kara Thistle.

She had been the fiancée of his best friend—they had all grown up together. Now she was a special agent for the FBI. Kara was the last person he expected to see walking back into his life, if even only professionally.

Time had treated her well enough, although she'd lost the softness of youth. Her cinnamon hair was scraped back in a no-nonsense ponytail at the base of her neck, and she wore neither earrings nor makeup. Her cheeks glowed from the salty sea air and clear, marble-green eyes stared back at him. A stunning young woman had blossomed into a striking adult, not that Matthew was surprised. Good looks had never been her problem.

"Matthew." Her voice gave away nothing of what she may have been feeling, but there was something behind her eyes that betrayed her for a split second. To her credit, she recovered quickly. He acknowledged her with a stiff nod, feeling awkward as hell at the unexpected reunion. She'd never show it, but he suspected she was just as uncomfortable, and he wasn't surprised when she didn't waste time chewing the fat over old times. That was just fine by him. The less time they had to spend in each other's company the better. "This is my partner Dillon McIntyre. We're part of the Child Abduction Rapid Deployment Team—CARD for short—assigned to the Babysitter cases," she explained as she handed Matthew a business card as a matter of protocol.

"A pleasure," her partner, Dillon, said, his clipped tone accentuated by the subtle British accent that only made his pretty-boy good looks all the more suspect in Matthew's opinion. "It's like tromping around in a meat

locker around here. Worse than San Francisco with its
infernal fog," he commented darkly. He pulled the lapels
of his black wool topcoat a little closer around his neck
before muttering, "I'm going to freeze my bollocks off
in this place. If I'd enjoyed this kind of weather I'd have
stayed in England."

Kara spared her partner a look that said *shut it,* and he
stalked off to talk with the officers canvassing the area.

"I apologize for my partner. He's a little on edge," she
said. Then added, "He quit smoking a few days ago and
he feels it's only fair that everyone around him is suffering
as much as he is."

Matthew offered a curt nod. He couldn't really care less
about her partner. He was too busy wondering why, of all
the agents in the bureau, it had to be her assigned to this
case. He'd rather eat nails than sit and play nice with Kara.
It wasn't as if she'd left on the best of terms. But even as
anger banked over the years started to flare bright again,
he knew now was not the time for what he wanted to say
to her. Snuffing his feelings until he could talk without
snarling, he focused on the case. "What do you mean by
Babysitter *cases?* Are you saying there's been more than
one abduction?"

Kara paused, then answered with caution. "It's possible
there have been other cases connected to this one. Has
anyone else been down here since you made the call to
the bureau?"

"No. Just my team of investigators."

"Good. Hold on, guys. I want to take a look," she said,
gesturing to the officers who were preparing the body bag.
Matthew was seemingly forgotten for the moment.

Oh, hell no. He didn't like being dismissed. Not by her,
not by anyone. Matthew quickly followed. "What are you
looking for?" he asked, noting the way her stare slowly

perused the body, missing nothing and stopping for long moments on the garish ligature marks marring the child's bone-white skin at her neck and wrists.

She didn't answer right away. Instead, she met her partner's stare and said in a grim tone, "Call the CARD Team. Let them know we found the Linney girl. And then call the task force. We need them here ASAP." She rose. To Matthew she said, "Thanks for making the call. The bureau appreciates your diligence."

He didn't need a pat on the head. "Thanks aren't necessary. Just doing my job."

"You have our appreciation, just the same." Kara flashed a brief smile, devoid of anything aside from professional courtesy and Matthew had to suppress a shiver that didn't come from the weather. Then, for a moment, he could have sworn he'd seen disappointment cross her features when she said with a sigh, "We were hoping for a different outcome this time." But it was gone in a heartbeat when she spoke again. "This is a sensitive case. High profile. The press is all over it. It won't be long before they catch wind that another body has been found. You might want to brief your Public Information Officer on what is acceptable to release and what is not—which is just about everything. My partner will go over the protocol with you, if you're unsure."

"That won't be necessary," Matthew said, annoyed at what he perceived was implied incompetence on their part. "We know how to play with the press."

"This isn't a game." She looked at him sharply. "I'd prefer if you didn't use analogies that belittle the situation."

"Calm down," he said gruffly. "I'm not belittling anything. I'm just saying we're not idiots and I don't appreciate you coming here and implying that we are just because we're not overpaid government employees."

She stiffened and looked to her partner, who had pulled his North Face beanie down low to cover his ears and flipped the collar of his jacket up to ward off the wind. "I'm heading back to the car. Call in the troops. You coming?" McIntyre asked, the look in his eyes plainly communicating it was time to stop nettling the locals.

"In a minute," she said.

"Suit yourself," McIntyre replied, and wasted little time in returning to the heat of the car. But Matthew distinctly heard him say something about someone being a stubborn ass and he wondered if he was referring to him or Kara.

Kara turned, her eyes sparking with contained irritation but before she could say whatever was on her mind, Oren walked over.

"Doc wants to know if we can move her yet," Oren said, giving Kara a short acknowledgment. "Kara. Been a long time."

Kara nodded. "Good to see you, Oren," she said quietly.

"Go ahead and wrap things up," Matthew said to Oren without waiting for Kara's permission. The older man said little and went to convey Matthew's instructions.

Under most circumstances, he didn't mind working with other agencies, feds included, but the idea of working under Kara—well, it just rubbed him the wrong way. And the fact that he knew he shouldn't let private matters intrude on a case only frustrated him more. Needing to put some space between them so he could clear his head, he started to walk away, but she grabbed him by the arm, her grip strong and unyielding.

"We need to get something straight, right now," she said, low and firm. "We have to work together even if neither of us like the idea. There is something bigger than our problem with each other at stake here. A little girl is dead. And she's not the first child to die. Two boys, Jason Garvin and Drake Nobles, have died in similar circumstances. If we don't find a way to stop this murderer, there will be more dead little girls and boys. Do you hear me? So drop the attitude or I will have you replaced with someone else in your department who isn't handicapped by personal history. Are we clear?"

Matthew slowly pulled his arm free, his gaze hardening on the woman he'd once thought he was falling in love with, and said, "Don't do that again."

"Don't make this more difficult than it already is."

"I'd say it's too late for that, wouldn't you?"

She straightened as if realigning her attitude. "Of course not. I can treat you with professional courtesy. The question is, can you do the same?"

Not to be outdone, Matthew smirked. "I'm just following your lead, Agent Thistle."

Kara smiled thinly. "If that's the case, let's start over," she said, taking a deep breath for emphasis. "I'll want to speak to your medical examiner as soon as he's had a chance to look at the body. We'll be setting up temporary lodging at the Jackson Creek Motel in town but you can call my cell when the M.E. is ready for me to come down."

"Fine."

She started to leave but stopped and turned. "And Matthew, one more thing…I'd appreciate it if you'd keep the private details of my past here in Lantern Cove exactly that. In the past."

She didn't wait for his reply, which was probably a good thing. Matthew wasn't in the mood to agree with anything Kara had to say. And that wasn't professional.

Biting back the hot words dancing on his tongue, he

dialed back the response and turned on his heel in the opposite direction, putting his mind back in gear when seeing Kara had made him feel spun out.

They weren't kids anymore. Kara was never the person he'd grown up thinking she was and damn it, no matter what she had to say, when this was all through, Matthew had a few things to say to her. Whether she liked it or not.

"You have a way with the locals," Dillon remarked with his signature wry humor, but Kara didn't find anything amusing about coming face-to-face with Matthew Beauchamp after all these years. It was all she could do to cling to her training. Seeing him had rattled her cage in the worst way. "Care to share what that was all about?" he asked.

"No."

He shivered and turned the heater on full blast. "Why not?"

Kara shot him a dark look. "This isn't story hour. I want to stay focused on the case. I got another call from Senator Nobles on my voice mail. How the hell did he know another body was found?"

"Politicians have their fingers in all sorts of pies. No telling where he got the information. Does it matter he knows?"

"Yeah, and he's all over my ass about it."

Dillon shrugged. "He's acting like any father who's lost his son. He just has more clout than most. And considerably more influential friends."

"I know, but he's squeezing pretty hard. My head feels ready to pop."

"That's why they pay you the big bucks."

She refrained from commenting. Pulling onto the main road, she headed for town. She'd known there was a possibility that she'd come into contact with Matthew when she learned they were going to Lantern Cove, but she never would've guessed that it would be ten times harder on her than she imagined it would be. Physically, he was different. Bigger. More muscle. But he still had that silent brooding thing going on that had always intrigued her when they were kids. Whereas Neal had been the joker in their group, Matthew had been the quiet yet guiding force that had kept them from carrying out some of the stupider ideas they'd hatched up as daredevil teens. Those startling blue eyes hadn't lost their brilliance and his thick black hair, although cut shorter than before, was only starting to gray at the temple. Handsome. That's the word *other* women might use to describe him. It was several moments before she realized Dillon was talking to her. Shaking her head, she apologized. "What were you saying? I zoned out for a minute."

"I noticed. Why don't you just tell me what's going on between you and this local chief. Get it off your chest so you can focus. You know I'm always up for a story, one with plenty of juicy details, so don't skimp on the good stuff."

"It's nothing."

"Look, blank-faced girl. Don't forget, before I was assigned to this unit I was in interrogation. I know when someone is lying. Even you."

The corner of her mouth tipped up and Dillon's brow lifted in encouragement. She shook her head and said with a shrug, "I grew up here. It's a small town. It's inevitable that I'd run into someone from my childhood. Matthew and I were friends growing up."

"He didn't seem all that friendly to me. In fact, when he saw it was you, he looked downright pissed off. What'd you do to earn a look like that?"

"Nothing happened. I moved away. He stayed."

"You two ever an item?"

She kept her eyes on the road. "No." Partially true. One night did not constitute a relationship. Bad judgment was more like it but no matter what, she couldn't regret that night.

Dillon regarded her with a silent, assessing stare that anyone else might've squirmed under but Kara allowed a tiny smile to play on her lips despite her growing fatigue. She'd definitely need more sleep if she was going to deal with Matthew on a regular basis. Finally, Dillon shook his head. "More bullshit. All right, just answer me this. Is he going to be a problem?"

"Of course not." Hoped not. No, she absolutely knew not. "Are you questioning my ability to do my job, Dillon?"

"Only if need be. I've never had to in the past but this guy has you jumpy...on edge. It's not like you. This case is too important to let anything cloud your judgment. I know I don't have to tell you that."

"So don't." She flashed him a bright smile that she didn't feel. "I'm fine. I'd tell you if I wasn't. I know what's at stake."

"So we're good, then?" Dillon asked.

"We're golden."

"Good. You're the best in your field. We need your 'A' game."

"Don't start with the sports analogies. They sound weird coming out of your mouth. Everything's under control."

Perhaps if she told herself that enough times, it would make it true. Her cell phone buzzed at her hip and she pulled it free to glance at the number. Director Colfax. Their boss. Damn it. She didn't want to talk to him just yet. Dillon read her expression easily.

"The cell reception in this place is terrible," he remarked. "Damn near spotty in some places," he added, and she agreed.

"I know. It's the trees. Messes up the line of sight on the cell towers." She smiled and let the call go to voice mail. She'd call him after she'd had a chance to talk to the M.E. Until then, Colfax would just have to wait.

An hour later while Dillon met with the incoming task force team, Kara went to the morgue. This part of the job was her least favorite, especially when it dealt with kids. She steeled herself for the inevitable sadness that followed when the coroner slid that little body out from its metal locker.

She acknowledged the coroner, a short man with a balding pate, and flashed her credentials. "Cause of death yet?" she asked.

"Petechial hemorrhages combined with the bruising around her neck point to asphyxiation," he answered, opening the locker and pulling the metal slab forward with the young girl on it. So young. Snuffed out in a blink.

Kara swallowed the lump in her throat and pulled her camera free as she gestured. "May I?"

"You're the boss."

She carefully detailed the marks left behind by Hannah Linney's tormentor and silently promised, just as she had with the other two victims of the Babysitter, to bring him to justice.

"Any sign of sexual trauma?"

"None."

She nodded and exhaled the breath she'd been holding. So far, neither of the Babysitter's victims had been sexually assaulted but serial killers sometimes varied their routine for reasons unknown.

Kara was drawn to Hannah's flaxen hair and couldn't

help but ache for the mother that had given birth with high hopes for her daughter only to have them end in such horrific circumstances. Somewhere a mother wept with a ragged heart, sobbing one word over and over. *Why?*

She cleared her throat with difficulty. "Was there anything with the body? A small piece of paper, anything at all?"

The coroner frowned in thought, then slowly shook his head. "Not that I'm aware of, but you could ask the chief for sure. He's heading this case personally. He'd have the crime scene photos."

In the first two cases the Babysitter left something behind. It was his sick way of letting the cops know that he was one step ahead. Laughing. Kara was certain something had been missed. She made a mental note to return to Wolf's Tooth first thing tomorrow morning.

Nodding to the coroner, she indicated she was finished and hurried from the room, anxious to get back to the motel and away from the fear that clotted in her heart whenever she thought of how vulnerable children were in the world.

It made her want to call home and talk to her nine-year-old daughter, just so she could hear Briana's voice and know that she was safe, unlike the poor children who had somehow gotten caught in the Babysitter's net.

Chapter 2

Matthew caught Kara leaving the morgue. His first instinct was to ignore her and keep walking, but there was something about her drawn expression that slowed his feet before he could form a different directive in his brain.

The minute she realized she was not alone in the hall, her features relaxed into the blank, professional mask that Matthew knew came from training and not from her true feelings. That intimate knowledge of her personally should have given him an edge but it just made him feel as if he'd trespassed somehow.

"Did you get what you needed?" He gestured toward the morgue.

"Yes." As an afterthought, she added, "Thanks."

"Enough with the 'thank yous,'" he said, narrowing his gaze. Tiny lines of fatigue bracketed her eyes—he hadn't noticed them before. *Shake it off. If the woman couldn't sleep, that was her problem.* "Listen, you and I both know

I was just being courteous. I don't need thank-yous. You're here to do a job and I'm here to help on my end. Everyone has the same goal—to catch this freak—and I'm not going to stand in the way of that."

She regarded him for a long moment and he wondered what was going through that mercurial mind. "Glad to hear it. Did you find anything unusual at the crime scene?" she asked, switching gears.

"Aside from a dead body?"

"Paper, fabric, wood chips that obviously didn't come from the area…anything like that?"

"No. Why?"

She shook her head. "I'll need to be apprised of any trace evidence that was collected. I'll want to send it to our labs for analysis," she said.

"Just make sure it makes it back when you're through."

"Of course. We don't do things sloppy."

"I'll have to take your word for it. And you didn't answer my question."

And she clearly didn't want to. She looked at him as if he were a nuisance with impertinent questions. She was definitely of the "need to know" camp and it was apparent he didn't share the same clearance. Finally, she answered briefly. "The killer left something behind in the first murders."

He shifted. The conversation he most wanted to have with her kept moving to the forefront of his mind, but he managed to keep on topic. "I've been following this case in the press—" She made an expression that said *who hasn't?* "It's getting quite the coverage but I don't remember that bit of information. Can't hardly open a newspaper without seeing something on the case. The press is having a field day with the grisly Babysitter nickname. How'd they come up with that one?"

She spared him a brief look, irritation in full bloom but he didn't know if it was directed at him or the media "Catch phrases and nicknames sell papers and boos' ratings," she said, disdain just under the surface. "And somehow…the press got a hold of information that was sensitive to the case."

"Such as?"

"In both cases the person watching over the child, a caregiver of some sort, was killed when the victim wa taken. So the press dubbed him the Babysitter Killer, which then was shortened to the Babysitter."

"Catchy," he murmured, wondering what kind o sick person did these kinds of things to kids and thei caregivers. "I knew when I saw the body it was that Linne girl. What made you think it was the Babysitter involve and not some other nut job with a thing for kids?"

"The evidence. The killer likes to tie them up, whic leaves distinct ligature marks on the skin." She sighe "Hannah had the same marks as the other two. And whe we find something left behind with a message, there wi be no doubt."

"No doubt?"

"No, there's not." She met his gaze squarely. "Nc one."

Her confidence was both impressive and bordering o smug. He found both irritating.

"I read that one of the victims, Drake Nobles, was th son of Senator Nobles?" When she jerked a short nod i the affirmative, he shook his head. He wouldn't want i be in her shoes. "Getting pressure yet?"

She stiffened. "No more than any other case. We don

place priority that way. Someone's out there, killing kids. That makes this case move to the top."

He smiled, knowing full well she was probably getting squeezed by her superior who was no doubt taking it from the senator, but he was amused by her attempt to appear otherwise. "Well, I'm sure it can't be easy being in your place. Head of the CARD Team assigned to this case. Kids dying on your watch. Must suck. Especially for someone who's as ambitious as you."

She swallowed and her eyes registered the veiled reference to her past, even if she didn't immediately jump back with an acidic retort as he'd hoped. Kara readjusted her camera bag and simply offered a perfunctory smile, one that she might give an annoying reporter, and said, "Well, you know, that's why they pay me the big bucks. Good night, Matthew." And then she stalked past him, taking great care not to make contact with him in any way—as if he had the plague or something.

He should've followed her lead and continued to his office but his gaze lingered as she walked the long hallway, past rows of plaques and pictures of past chiefs hung on the walls, her shiny black boots clicking softly on the old tiled and dingy floor. Shoulders stiff as hardened plastic, she gave little indication of her mood except for the subtle yet angry twitch and sway of her hips. He suppressed a chuckle for no other reason than he recognized he'd delivered a low blow for selfish reasons and it didn't feel right to enjoy it so much. But it felt good. Bad as it was. After what she did to Neal...well, it's a damn miracle he didn't toss her from the Widow's Bridge and be done with it.

One could dream...he sighed and walked to his office to finish his paperwork for the night.

Kara got back to the motel, still fuming. What a passive-aggressive prick. Why didn't he just come out and say what was on his mind? Obviously, it was killing him to hold it back, and instead of getting it off his chest so they could all focus on the job, he kept slipping in little jabs at her expense.

"Must suck," she mimicked under her breath as she unlocked the motel room door and slammed it behind her. And how did he know all that about her? She placed her camera on the bed and jerked off her overcoat. A light blinked on the phone indicating she had a message waiting. She lifted the receiver and retrieved the message, sighing when it was Colfax again. He'd already left two voice mails on her cell.

A soft knock at the front door and Dillon walked in a second later. She replaced the receiver. "I could've been naked," she said, pulling her cell phone free from its holster at her hip. "Try waiting until I answer, will you?"

"And miss a chance to catch you in your birthday suit? Never." He gestured toward the phone. "That Colfax?"

"Yeah. He call you?"

"Yes. I told him you were too busy fighting with the local chief to take his calls but you'd get back to him as soon as you were able."

She glared, even though she knew he would never say such a thing to their director. "You're lucky I know you're kidding. You know that British humor…it's a hit and miss thing with Americans. Most of the time we just don't get it."

"No, *you* don't get it because *you* don't have a sense of humor."

"Ha-ha. Are you here to bust my balls or do you have something useful to share?"

"Actually, I do. The fax came from Dr. Benton, that geologist from Davis University we sent the mineral sample to."

That got her attention. "And?"

"And it seems maybe our killer is from your own backyard. The mineral found on the body of the Garvin boy is called orickite. It's a sulphide and it's only found around these parts. Do you know of any active mines close by?"

"No, but we can certainly find out." She started for the phone but then remembered Lantern Cove pretty much shut down after five. "Are the rest of the team settled in?"

Dillon nodded. "Four rooms booked down the hall, all federal agents. You want me to get them rounded up for a meeting? I thought we'd meet first thing in the morning over a spot of breakfast, preferably something hot to keep the hypothermia at bay."

"Smart-ass. And, no. Go ahead and bring them over now. You and I are going for a hike tomorrow."

"A hike?" Dillon's brow arched. "What kind of hike? I don't know if I brought the right wardrobe for that sort of excursion."

"We're going back to the crime scene. In the first two murders, the killer left something behind. Matthew's team didn't find anything but I know the killer left his signature calling card. We have to find it."

"We haven't concluded that what you're thinking of as clues were actually left behind by the killer. There was no DNA on the paper found near the Garvin boy and it was printed on a computer so we can't even get a handwriting analysis."

Kara shook her head. "It wasn't random. He wants us to think that it is but there's no reason a child would carry around something like that." She met his dubious stare. "I'm right about this. I can feel it."

"You're the boss," Dillon said with a sigh. "What time tomorrow?"

"At 7:00 a.m."

He groaned. "Just because you're an insomniac doesn't mean the rest of us are."

"At 7:00 a.m.," she repeated. "Not a minute later." The corner of her mouth twitched. "Now, go call the team. I want to get this briefing underway before everyone starts trying to claim overtime."

By the time the briefing was over and everyone had returned to their rooms for the night, Kara felt an all-over body fatigue and actually welcomed the thought of sinking into the motel bed.

She rose on legs stiff from sitting in one position too long. After washing her face and throwing on some pajamas, she climbed into the bed and gratefully closed her eyes. Perhaps tonight she'd be able to sleep without the details of the case she was working scrolling across her brain in rapid succession, screaming for closure, demanding everything she had and then some.

But even as she started to drift into slumber, a memory, buried deep, surfaced and she rolled onto her side as if to escape it.

Summer, 1990. She, Neal and Matthew were driving to the beach…the smell of her coconut suntan lotion filled the truck's cabin…the sound of their laughter mingled with the music of Aerosmith…she felt safe, flanked by the two boys.

Then, as dreams often do, the scene changed without warning to the night before she left. The fight. The words that were said that couldn't be taken back. The heavy weight of regret and guilt that she carried each time she looked into her daughter's eyes.

Matthew's eyes.

Kara tossed. The dream faded but the feeling that she'd lost something precious remained. Just as it always did.

Her eyes cracked open a slit but slid closed again. For once sheer exhaustion overruled everything else. And she was grateful.

The next morning was much like the day Hannah's body was found, only bleaker as dark storm clouds gathered on the horizon and headed straight for Lantern Cove. Angry waves crashed against the inland rocky shores as the wind picked up and howled through the trees.

If Kara were the superstitious sort, she'd say there was an uneasy energy coursing through the air. But she certainly didn't believe in that crap, nor would she admit to the shiver that ricocheted down her spine as she waited for Dillon.

"Picked a cherry of a day to go hiking," he said, locking his door and pocketing his key. "If it rains, we'll lose whatever trace you're hoping to find."

Kara looked to the sky and nodded grimly. "I know. We should get a move on. Maybe we can beat the rain."

Dillon shook his head. "I don't know, but we can try. Oh, by the way, I left a voice mail for Beauchamp to let him know we were going out there," he said as they climbed into Kara's Range Rover.

She looked at him sharply. "Why'd you do that? We don't need his permission."

"No, but it's a professional courtesy and you know it. Why are you so set on making an enemy of this guy?"

Too late for that. Kara opened her mouth but snapped it shut, knowing that if she let fly what had popped into her head it would only open the door for more discussion about her past. She wasn't interested in doing that. "You're right. Sorry. I need coffee."

"No problem. There's a coffee shop along the way."

"Good." She looked to Dillon. "I didn't mean to snap. This place combined with the case…it's got me on edge."

He accepted her answer but then said with a cheerfulness that was unnatural that early in the morning, "Well, since you're already grouchy, I should let you know that Beauchamp called me back after I left a voice mail. Seems he keeps the same late hours as you, fancy that. He said he'd meet us out there."

She jerked to face Dillon. "What?"

Dillon shrugged. "Figured another pair of eyes wouldn't hurt. Besides, he knows the area."

"I know the area," Kara said, trying not to grit her teeth. "We don't need Beauchamp."

"You *used* to know the area. You've been gone a long time. A lot can change. Honestly, Thistle, what the hell is wrong with you? You've never gotten so bent about working with the locals before. Besides, it only makes sense to add him to the task force. What's wrong?"

Kara shoved the gearshift into Drive. "Nothing."

"There you go lying again. You have the most entertaining tic in your eye—minute, really—when you lie through your teeth. Good fun to watch under most circumstances but this morning I'm not really in the mood—so just get on with it and spill already."

"We just don't get along." That much was obvious. "Why would I want him tagging along?" Kara snapped, then hearing her own shrewish tone, she tried again. "I mean, I don't want anything to distract me from the job and if I have a surly police chief to deal with, I might miss something crucial."

"Be that way. There's more to it. But you're obviously

determined to be a horse's ass about the whole thing. So piss off with you, then."

Thank goodness for small favors. The ensuing silence allowed her to shake loose the tight feeling in her chest that constricted her lungs the minute Dillon mentioned Matthew. She worried her bottom lip until she realized she was doing it and quickly stopped. She glanced at Dillon. "I was engaged to his best friend, Neal," she said, breaking the silence reluctantly.

"You, engaged? Pardon me for a minute while I suspend my disbelief." He paused a minute as if mentally switching gears and just as she was tempted to throw him out of her car while driving at a high rate of speed, he continued. "So what happened?"

"He died."

"Before or after you broke off the engagement?"

She startled. "How'd you know it was me that broke it off?"

Dillon's smile was slow and just smug enough to ride the edge of annoying. "I know you. You're a heartbreaker, not the heartbroken."

That's where Dillon was wrong. Her heart had been broken, she was just adept at shoving the shattered pieces into a dusty corner. "He died after."

"How'd he die?"

Kara pursed her lips, not quite sure she wanted to share the rest. She worked very hard to keep those details from crowding her on a daily basis. Dillon was prodding her relentlessly, so she relented but kept to the barest of facts, as if she were relating details of a case instead of pieces of her past.

"He wanted me to stay in Lantern Cove. I'd just been accepted into the bureau. I had to go. He didn't agree. We parted ways and unfortunately, a month later he died in a car accident. Can we drop it now? The memories aren't pleasant and I try not to go there anymore."

"Fair enough."

She focused on the drive to Wolf's Tooth and soon they were there.

Matthew was waiting. He stood casually against his Jeep Cherokee, his expression inscrutable, his breath curling in the cold.

They exited the car. Kara nodded to Matthew. "Thanks for meeting us," she offered, even if she didn't mean it.

"So what do you think my team missed?"

"Like I mentioned earlier, with both of the past victims, the killer left behind a small clue. Something that in overgrown, wooded terrain might easily get missed if the investigator didn't know what to look for."

"Such as?" His expression darkened even as she knew his mind was working quickly.

"Something with a message. With the Garvin boy, it was a slip of paper tucked into a pocket. On Drake Nobles, it was one of those candy hearts with a printed message. At first we thought it was random, some weird little quirk, but I soon realized he was baiting us. Mocking us. He doesn't think he's going to get caught."

Matthew pushed off the vehicle, his tone all business. "Let's do it. The rain is coming and that bastard *is* getting caught."

The three started the climb down into Wolf's Tooth, for the second time in as many days, the cold biting into her skin while brambles scratched and grabbed, and Kara remembered why she'd never enjoyed hiking.

Kara slid the final few feet and if Matthew hadn't caught her, his strong grip closing around her waist, she would've fallen flat on her butt, or worse, gone tumbling head over heels.

"Watch your step," he said. Electricity sparked between them with the accidental contact and Kara stopped the immediate gasp that nearly flew from her mouth.

"Thanks," she muttered, stepping away from him.

His gaze swept over her but he didn't say anything else, just turned and kept walking. "This way."

They walked twenty more feet before they reached the area where Hannah's body was found and Dillon said he was going to canvas the perimeter, leaving Kara and Matthew to search the underbrush.

The foliage, dense and varied shades of green, was damp from the misty weather. A distant crack of thunder heralded the coming storm.

"He kept her alive for a few days," Matthew said, without breaking his careful search. He looked up. "Did he do that with his other victims?"

It was one of the details that bothered Kara the most. Each time a child went missing, that short window of time seemed to taunt them for they knew it wasn't long enough to find them. The killer knew it, too. "Yes. He's a sadist. He wants to enjoy their pain."

"You keep referring to the killer as a he. Is there something you know that you're not saying?"

"No. Statistically, serial killers are men. I don't care if it's a man or a woman. Either way, he or she is going down. I think it's just easier sometimes for me to think of him as a man."

A ghost of a smile crossed his lips but it was gone in a heartbeat. "Why? Because it's hard to believe a woman would do something so awful to a child?"

She met his gaze and answered truthfully. "Yes."

"Who knew…Kara Thistle has a soft spot after all."

She scowled, realizing her mistake. "I'm going to check over there. Holler if you find something."

Kara made her way carefully through the underbrush, noting every detail of the terrain, looking for some kind of sign that the killer had screwed up and left behind more than just a discarded body. She glanced back at Matthew, his solid form moving through the dense forest ground cover, and wondered if there'd ever come a day when those blue eyes didn't smolder with hatred when they focused on her.

Not likely. An unexpected burn behind her eyes caught her off guard. She wiped at them with an impatient motion, irritation blooming at her own lack of control just because she was around Matthew again. What was wrong with her?

"Hey, I think I found something."

Moving briskly, she pulled a glove from her pocket and slipped it on as she went. "What have you got?"

Matthew pointed at a tiny slip of paper, barely noticeable under the wide green fern fronds, as a corner stuck out from under the earth.

"Dillon," she called out. "Over here!"

Bending down, she gently moved the dirt so she could pull the paper free. Her heartbeat slowed to a painful thud as she scanned the damp slip.

"Mulberry bush," Kara read, her brow furrowing as she handed it over to Dillon to put into an evidence bag.

"Isn't that part of a nursery rhyme?" Dillon asked.

"All around the mulberry bush, the monkey chased the weasel," she answered softly, then looked at Matthew. "What do you think it means?"

"I don't know but I don't like it. I've always thought there was a certain creep factor to most of the old nursery rhymes," Matthew said, frowning.

"Why?"

Matthew looked at her. "Because they never mean

what they say. They're too cloak and dagger for my tastes. Besides, haven't you ever noticed that a lot of those rhymes are kind of violent toward kids?"

Dillon agreed. "I think the chief is right. Perhaps the bastard is using the rhyme as a metaphor."

"A metaphor for what?" Matthew asked.

"I haven't a clue," Dillon answered, shrugging. "But it can't be literal, now can it? I don't suspect the killer keeps a pet monkey or weasel for kicks. I suppose we'll have to do some research on the blasted nursery rhyme."

"Great. Someone who fancies himself clever. Just what we need," Kara said, rubbing her temple. "All right, Dillon, see if anything turns up in the origin of the rhyme."

Matthew's jaw hardened and Kara knew he was fighting against his urge to grind his teeth. When he spoke again, his tone was ominous. "We haven't seen the last of this guy. My gut tells me he's on the prowl for his next victim."

Kara agreed, shivering and blaming the cold, which was already causing her teeth to chatter. As if on cue, the rain started and Kara was only too happy to get out of that ravine. There was a sadness that clung to the area, as if Hannah's spirit was lingering, waiting for someone to solve her murder and prevent more from meeting the same fate.

She looked back as they climbed up the steep grade and for a split second she could've sworn she'd actually seen someone standing there. Kara blinked. Nothing but hundred-year-old trees and undergrowth remained.

Tricks of the mind, she thought shakily. Tricks of the mind.

Chapter 3

It was late and the storm that had started when they were down in the ravine was pelting the earth with fat, angry raindrops, creating a staccato against the tiled roof of the single-story motel. She'd declined to go out with the team for a bite to eat, preferring to go over case notes and forensic reports, though as she glanced at her watch and her stomach growled in complaint she wondered if maybe she should've chosen differently. Sighing, she fished a can of salted almonds from her bag and popped the top. *Voila, dinner.*

Tossing a few into her mouth, she'd just settled into the chair with her pad and pencil when a short rap at the door had her tensing. The team hadn't returned yet, which made whoever was on the other side of that door, suspect. Moving softly and grabbing her gun, she called out, "Who is it?"

There was a pause and then she heard Matthew answer. "Me. I, uh, brought you something."

Puzzled, she holstered her gun and opened the door a crack. Matthew stood there with a bag of Chinese takeout, his expression hard to read. Glancing down at her wardrobe, she grimaced at the tight, long-sleeved sleep shirt and soft flannel pants she was wearing. Well, it'd been a long time but Matthew had certainly seen her in less, so she reluctantly opened the door wider. "For me?"

He lifted the plastic bag from Mr. Choy's. "Mu shu chicken. Used to be your favorite. I ran into your team as I was picking up my order and McIntyre told me you'd stayed behind. Figured you ought to eat something," he added a bit gruffly as if he were just as surprised as she was at his actions. He reached into the bag and pulled out the mu shu, thrusting it at her. "So here. Take it or leave it. Hell, I don't even know if you even like this stuff anymore."

She accepted the container and the sweet, tangy smell teased her senses, kicking her suppressed appetite awake with a vengeance. "I do. Thanks. Do you…want to come in?" she asked, unsure.

Matthew hesitated, then stepped over the threshold as she closed the door behind him. She took a seat at the small table where her notes were strewn about in a haphazard mess that belied her generally organized nature. Moving a few of her piles, she cleared a space for him to join her. "I can't believe Mr. Choy's is still in business after all these years," she said, making small talk as she dug into the still-warm order. She chewed slowly, enjoying the pleasure of a once-favorite food. "He was old when I left."

Matthew opened his own container of sweet-and-sour pork and, before digging in, said, "His boy took over. Does a pretty good job of picking up where his old man left off.

Mr. Choy, from what I hear, is loving retirement and has taken a shine to golf, despite being near to ninety years old."

"At least he's staying active," she murmured, taking another bite. She gestured with her fork to the food. "It's great. You're right. Tastes as good as I remember, so his son must be doing a bang-up job."

They ate in silence but Kara knew they were both thinking the same thing: in what universe was it possible that she and Matthew were sitting at the same table, eating dinner like old friends? She swallowed and glanced at him surreptitiously, her practiced eye noting every detail about his appearance that was different and yet the same.

Solid Matthew. Always the practical one. The phantom of a smile threatened to play on her lips as she thought of the numerous scrapes and binds they'd narrowly escaped as kids simply because they'd had the sense to at least listen to Matthew when things had gone too far. It was a miracle nothing had ever managed to make it to her permanent record, a boon she no doubt owed to Matthew, not Neal. Often Neal had been as headstrong and reckless as she in their teens. Her daughter, Briana, had inherited that quiet wisdom Matthew had come by so naturally. For that, Kara was grateful.

Finished, she pushed her container away and sighed at her full belly. She didn't often get the opportunity to just sit and eat without feeling pressured to finish so she could return to the task she'd set aside.

"Thanks. That hit the spot," she said, her gaze roaming his face as she looked for clues into his motivation. For as much as she wanted to enjoy this unexpected gesture of kindness, she didn't trust it for a minute.

He shrugged. "Can't think on an empty stomach, right? I remember you used to get light-headed when you didn't eat. Wouldn't want you to keel over at an inopportune moment." His gaze met hers in a speculative manner as he cocked his head. "Looks to me that you don't eat enough these days. You've gotten skinny."

"And you've bulked up," she countered, although she refrained from adding that his bulk came from muscle not fat and that it made his six-foot-plus frame all the more impressive.

His mouth twitched as he laced his fingers across his solid abdominal region, which she imagined sported a full six-pack underneath that dark thermal Henley. "True. I like to eat so I have to work out."

No ring. Her gaze bounced from his bare fingers, and she hoped he didn't notice, but such luck was too much to ask for.

"Just ask."

She started to give him her best blank stare, as if she didn't know what he was saying, but dropped the ruse when curiosity won out over prudence. "Married?"

"No."

"Never?"

"I didn't say that."

Kara chuckled, yet an odd pain punched her in the side, suspiciously close to her heart. "What happened?"

The blue in his eyes darkened but the casual lift of his shoulders told a different story. "Just didn't work out. Sort of like you and Neal, I guess. Except, my ex-wife is still alive and living quite comfortably on the alimony I pay her."

"Neal and I never actually made it to the altar," she reminded him quietly.

"Yes, I remember. I was supposed to be his best man."

She refused to wince at his statement and instead quietly

tucked away the fact that he hadn't mentioned child support. And she was inordinately happy. Dangerous thinking, she silently reprimanded herself even as she pulled away and started to clean up the food containers. "Well, everything happens for a reason, right?"

"That's what some people say." He handed her his trash. "How about you?"

She dropped the trash into the canister, making a mental note to put the can outside of the room for the cleaning staff to empty first thing tomorrow. She didn't allow them to clean due to the sensitive nature of her stay. The busy work made for an easy excuse to stall but Matthew knew her well, even if years stood between them.

"What have you been doing with your life all these years? I don't see a ring on your finger, either."

She pushed a lock of hair behind her ears. "I'm married to the job."

"I can see that. Top of your field, the go-to person in high-profile cases...you've done well for yourself. But there's more to life than the job, right?"

Kara bit the inside of her cheek, her daughter's beloved little face jumping to mind, and she had to stop the smile that would've followed. Briana was the light in her universe, the one bright spot in an otherwise depressing world. But Matthew was the last person she wanted to know about Briana—even if she was his daughter.

Somehow she didn't think he'd understand. Matthew had never been the type to forgive and forget. He'd still not forgiven her for leaving Lantern Cove and breaking Neal's heart in the process.

No, she thought sadly, Matthew would never know that the one night they both betrayed Neal had resulted in a wonderful little girl. And that was for the best—for everyone.

Breaking her reflective silence, she met Matthew's stare with a short smile. "The job is enough for me."

His own smile turned wintry. "Well, we both know you sacrificed a lot to get where you're at."

"Yes, I have." *More than you know.* "And on that note…I'm going to have to say good night. Thanks for the food."

Matthew went to the door. "Don't mention it," he murmured. And then he was gone.

Kara brushed her teeth and finally climbed into bed, her eyelids feeling weighted with cement, which was a welcome feeling. Working herself to exhaustion was the only way she ever got any sleep, especially when she was under the gun to catch the bad guy.

She couldn't have been asleep long before something jerked her awake with the certainty that she wasn't alone.

Pitch-black filled the room. Without adjusting her position, she peered into the darkness, managing to keep her breathing slow and steady as if she were still asleep, but she could discern nothing. Confused, she slowly sat up in the bed, and flicked on the bedside lamp.

Nothing. Her room was exactly as it was when she went to sleep. Rubbing the grit from her eyes, she sighed and chalked it up to extreme fatigue. Snapping off the light, she fell back against her pillow and closed her eyes, determined to catch more *zzzz's* before her alarm went off at 6:00 a.m. Just then, a soft voice whispered in her ear and nearly stopped her heart.

"She's here."

Chapter 4

Kara's head ached and her skin itched.

"What's wrong?" Dillon asked from above the rim of his coffee cup. "You look like shit."

She ignored him for the moment and took a bracing swallow of her own coffee—black without sugar—before attempting an answer. The hot brew burnt the crap out of her tastebuds but oddly the flash of pain was more welcome than the uneasy thoughts making soup of her brain. "Just because you say that with an accent doesn't make it any less insulting."

Dillon made a face. "Someone's gone into mommy-mode. Next are you going to tell me that if I've got nothing nice to say I should—"

"Shut the hell up?" she provided with a false smile.

"Something like that. I seem to remember that saying being a little less acerbic and more polite but that certainly gets the point across. So, what's with the nerves?

You're drumming your thumbs," he pointed out, which immediately made her slide her hands under the table away from view. "Something's got you strung pretty tight. What is it?"

She could try and pass it off as extreme fatigue—hell, she'd been trying to do that since 4:00 a.m.—but it was no use. Someone had whispered in her ear. *She's here.* And yet, her room had been empty. How the hell was she supposed to say that without looking as if she'd just spilled her crackers? "I didn't sleep well," she said, leaving it at that.

"Not me. I slept like a baby. This motel sure doesn't look like much from the outside—in fact, it looks like the kind of place where the crazed proprietor slits your throat in your sleep—but in all, the beds are quite adequate."

"I'm glad to hear you're bright-eyed and bushy-tailed," she said wryly, choking down another hot swallow as she started to feel the caffeine working its way into her body, clearing away the cobwebs of sleep until she felt somewhat back to herself. It was a dream, she rationalized with a great deal of relief. A very lucid, very vivid dream. Not uncommon for people who are extremely fatigued. Now she felt just a little ridiculous for wasting so much of her precious sleep time shaking in her bed over something that was clearly not real.

Just in time. The rest of the CARD Team came into the small breakfast joint and Kara was grateful for the need to focus on the job.

D'Marcus Jones, the high-tech computer specialist who looked as far from a geek as one could get, slid into the seat beside her while Tana Miller and Zane Harris took the seats flanking Dillon. Everyone except Tana signaled for coffee. Tana preferred green tea and always brought her own. All she required was a mug of steaming hot water.

"Does it always rain like this here?" D'Marcus asked, eyeing the dismal weather with something of a scowl. "I feel like I'm gonna mold or something. Even the sheets felt damp."

"I think it's invigorating," Tana said, her cheeks still pink from the early-morning run she'd taken on the black-sand beach a short walk from their motel. "I could live here."

Kara withheld comment. The beaches here were savagely beautiful with sharp, craggy cliffs that accepted the ocean's constant battering with stoic dignity, eroding with time until deep fissures ran with seawater as the spray erupted with a violent explosion against the rocks. Many a tourist, inexperienced with the nature of Northern California's coastal beaches, sank to a watery grave when they turned their back to the ocean.

And it wasn't warm. Not even in the summer. The water remained a chilly temperature and dive suits were necessary if prolonged exposure was planned. But Kara never went into the ocean. Not after her dad took a fishing boat into a squall after a bender and never came back. It'd been her senior year. Neal's family had taken her in so she could graduate.

"Didn't you grow up here?" D'Marcus asked, pouring two creams into his white ceramic mug.

"Yes." How many times had she wished she'd been born somewhere other than the Emerald Triangle, the place where marijuana grows as freely as the foxglove? More times than she could count. She'd never truly fit in with the locals—but she was one. "Let's get this meeting started," she said briskly, ending the invitation for story hour or trips down Memory Lane. "The weather is likely to get worse before it gets better and if you don't want to spend the entire day wet *and* puking your guts out, we'd better get a move on."

"What's this puking part?" D'Marcus asked, his dark brows drawn in a troubled line. "I don't like the sounds of that."

"You know the road from Willits to Westport?" Kara asked, and D'Marcus nodded warily. "Well, the roads we're going on will put that road to shame. Ten-mile-an-hour switchbacks, seven percent grade…you might want to take some Dramamine before we head out. We're going deep into the redwoods today."

"We who? I thought we're staying here to set up the command center while you and that police chief guy are going out to the backwoods?"

Kara startled. "What? Who said *that?*" She shot a look at Dillon, who returned her hard stare with a nonchalant one that made her want to strangle the shit out of him. She'd enjoy watching his eyeballs pop out like little marbles and roll around on the floor. Then she'd stomp on them. Little sneaky Brit.

"Listen, don't get your panties in a twist. I called the police station, looking for a trail guide, so's we don't get lost in the heathen beauty of this place you used to call home and get our heads shot off by one of the hippie locals because we stumbled on their retirement plan. Lucky for us, the chief volunteered."

"We don't need him," she said, brushing off Dillon's idea quickly. She was not spending all day tromping around the forest with Matthew. She suppressed a shiver that wasn't entirely born of distaste and ignored Dillon's expression. "D'Marcus, you can come with me. Chief Beauchamp can worry about his own investigations. I'm sure he has plenty to do without horning in on ours."

"Actually, I agree with Dillon," D'Marcus interrupted.

"He knows the area, he's got the authority to squelch any problems with the locals and I'm betting he doesn't get carsick. Dramamine makes me tired. You know I can't take that stuff and use my brain at the same time. It's better if I stay behind at the command center. Besides, that new equipment is coming in and I need to be here to get it set up."

"So it's settled, then?" Dillon said casually. "You and the chief will go. Great. I'm starved. What's good here?"

"It's not settled," she snapped, startling the team with her tone. *Count to ten. Get a grip. Stop letting Matthew get under your damn skin!* Mentally giving herself a slap upside the head, she forced a shrug. "Fine." But then she offered Dillon a mean smile as she said, "But you get to interview the locals while I'm gone." She rose from the table, her appetite all but gone. "I'd suggest you start with Tally's at the Pier, and if you order anything, try the catch of the day. It's...*delicious.*"

If Dillon knew her at all, her tone was saying the opposite.

"Not much of a fish guy," Dillon said. He knew her well. "But thanks anyway."

"Don't mention it," Kara said sweetly, and after everyone was clear on their assignments, she left the diner.

Acid churning in her stomach, she tried to keep focused but with the lack of sleep and her nerves stretched taut as piano wire, it was a futile effort. Returning to her room, she closed the door behind her and sagged against it. Flipping her cell phone, she hit the speed dial for home and waited for the familiar voice of Mai, Briana's Vietnamese nanny, to pick up. After four rings, it went to voice mail. Only mildly troubled, for there were multiple reasons why Mai or Briana might not pick up, she sighed and pocketed her cell phone without leaving a message. She'd try again tonight when she'd be more likely to catch them.

She walked to the table where her notes were strewn and studied the case files of each victim with a slow and methodical style, going over every detail as if they weren't already etched into her memory. A soft, distressed sound escaped her lips. So young. The nightmare started with Jason Garvin, son of an architectural drafting professor at Washington University. At that point they had no idea there'd be more. It had seemed a random abduction by a stranger—a crime of opportunity. But then, not long after, Drake Nobles, the son of California senator Peter Nobles was taken and found, mere days later, with the same ligature marks as the previous victim. Kara had known then with an uncomfortable certainty that they had a serial killer on the loose. Unfortunately, that was also the point when the case had been catapulted into the public eye and she'd been tapped as the official spokesperson for the CARD Team. Kara hated the spotlight, preferring to work in the shadows, quietly and efficiently getting things done, but Director Colfax had wanted her front and center for reasons that chafed.

And now the most recent victim, Hannah Linney, the daughter of an assistant district attorney in San Francisco, had disappeared last week when she was last seen walking home from school with her nanny. The nanny's body had been discovered in an alley by the school and all trace of Hannah was gone. Kara flipped through the crime scene photos. Hannah had been a fighter. There was evidence that she'd scratched and clawed her assailant, although no DNA was found under her nails. They'd been scraped clean postmortem. Whoever had taken these children knew enough to leave nothing behind other than what they wanted found.

Aside from the first case, the other two were snatched in California. There was nothing to tie them together. At least nothing she could see. But she was sure there was something. The *Babysitter* fancied himself clever. Her lip curled. She hated that term, which had been coined by the media. Now she was using it, as well. Her stomach growled and she tossed back a few stale almonds left over from last night. It's no wonder she couldn't keep any weight on, she thought, recalling Matthew's comment about her figure. This kind of work would kill anyone's appetite.

A knock at the door drew her attention and she instinctively knew it was Matthew, but she approached the door with caution just the same.

"Who is it?"

"It's me."

Her stomach tensed as anxiety twisted her nerves but she'd die before she'd let Matthew know just how much he put her on edge.

Chapter 5

The low rumble of Matthew's voice sounded from the other side of the door, and with a silent prayer for resilience, she opened it with her best I'm-a-professional smile. Perfunctory is what she was trying for but for all the attention he gave her, the effort was moot.

"Ready?"

No hello, how are you, good morning—just all business. *Perfect, just the way it should be,* she told herself, as she gathered her maps and notebook and stuffed them into her hiking backpack. "Just waiting for you."

"Let's get going then," he said, and turned on his heel. "The roads are going to be slop by the time we get up the mountain."

"You don't have to go…if you have other things you need to do," she said, hurrying after him, the rain pelting her hat as if it were trying to pummel her brain. "It's not exactly great weather. I'd understand if you wanted to find someone else to take me out to the mine."

"You want someone else to take you? I could get Oren or Dinky to take you up there."

He turned to face her and she stared at him, wavering on taking him up on his offer, but then she pictured the stone-faced Oren and the doofus Dinky and she knew her best option—if not her favorite—would be with Matthew. "No. You're already here. Let's go."

"All right then," he said and climbed into the older model Jeep Cherokee. "Fasten your seat belt," he instructed, and she sent him an irritated look. *I'm not a kid*. He shrugged. "The Kara I remember liked to break the rules," he said by way of explanation, if that's what you could call it.

She huffed and jerked the belt across her chest. "I'm not that girl anymore."

Matthew's hand rested on the gearshift and he briefly assessed her with those killer blue eyes. Kara forced herself to hold his stare without flinching or giving away any indication that his presence knocked her sidewise.

Finally, Matthew put the car into Drive as he said, "No, I guess you're not. Sorry."

"Fine," she said, accepting the apology, yet her chest felt tight and it seemed hard to breathe around whatever was sitting on her chest. How could she have not realized just how much Briana and Matthew looked alike? She was his carbon copy, down to the serious light in her ocean-blue eyes, to the quiet intelligence that she showed with everything she did. Kara thought of the small picture she had on the motel nightstand beside her bed and sweat broke out on her brow. If Matthew saw that picture, he'd know. There'd be no wondering. Knowledge would be immediate and the careful world she'd built for Briana and herself would shatter.

"Something wrong?" he asked.

"No."

Matthew knew she was lying. Kara's palms began to sweat. She rubbed her thighs and looked out the window, eager to focus on anything but the close proximity of the man beside her.

"It's hard to be around each other," he acknowledged quietly. "I think we can admit that without hurting each other's feelings."

She looked at him sharply. "Matthew, the case has me on edge. Not you."

He stiffened and she could nearly feel him physically shutting her out, slamming the door on any fledgling attempt at civility, and she was alternately relieved and horrified. Shame. That's the feeling that was crushing her. God, she was ashamed for not having the courage to tell him that he had a daughter. Ashamed to realize that she may have been wrong to keep them apart. She'd been reacting to the situation at the time and figured this was best, but perhaps it had only been best for her. But what the hell could she do about it now? Nothing. So it would remain the same. She'd deal. She had to.

"How far to Wilkin's Mine?" she asked, keeping her voice professional, businesslike.

"An hour."

An hour. *Fabulous.* She imagined having a Brazilian bikini wax would be less painful than sitting in a car with Matthew suffering through stilted, awkward conversation as they each navigated around the emotional land mines that could blow them both to bits. "Music?" she asked, moving to turn the stereo on.

"Not interested in catching up?" he asked as she turned the volume up. His mouth twisted knowingly with just a touch of mocking cruelty. "Guess not."

She shot him a dark look and then returned to the scenery outside her window. In spite of the rain that continued to fall from the gray skies, the melancholy beauty of the coastal forests was something that tugged at her emotional center. It was hard to ignore that her roots were here, even as much as she tried. It was probably why she'd requested the San Francisco office. She needed to hear the ocean and smell the briny perfume of the sea. Her family had always been attached to the water. Her father had been a fisherman just like his father before him. Some of her best memories included the sea. In spite of herself, Kara wondered if Matthew still enjoyed abalone diving, or if he had ever bought that sailboat he'd been wanting when they were kids. Probably not. Neal had been the impulsive, spontaneous one. Matthew always weighed the pros and cons of everything six ways from Sunday before he did something. She shifted in her seat, uncomfortable with the nostalgia plucking memories from her mental chest that she'd locked away long ago.

Regret tasted metallic on her tongue. She risked a glance at his profile. Strong, stubborn jaw, lips compressed to a tight line, betraying some kind of inner conflict as did the pull of his dark brows shadowing his eyes. Likely, if she'd told Matthew about their daughter, he would've taught her to dive, to enjoy and respect the ocean. He would've taught Briana to play guitar. She swallowed as she recalled Briana's most recent request.

"Why didn't you have kids?" she asked, glancing at him curiously. "When you were married, I mean."

"Back to catching up?" he asked, the mild tone deceptive.

She shrugged. "It's a long drive. You don't have to answer of course. I was just wondering."

The frown eased as he considered his answer. Finally,

he admitted, "I did want kids. She didn't. Takes two to make that happen. Seeing as how things turned out, it was for the best. How about you?"

"My job."

He seemed to accept that. Of course he did. It made sense. Her job was chaotic with odd, often-times long hours. Adding a child to the mix would certainly be difficult. And it was. If it weren't for the treasure that Mai had turned out to be…single parenting wasn't for wimps.

The shame returned. He'd wanted children. A moment of insanity gripped her and she imagined just blurting out that he had a child. A wonderful, beautiful, smart and amazing kid who looked just like him and even had that same stubborn tilt of the chin. Yeah…that would go over well. The breath hitched in her chest as she discarded the dangerous thought and returned to the case.

"Tell me again about the photographer who found Hannah Linney."

"He's already been checked out. His alibi is airtight. There's no way he dropped that little girl out there. Tell me why we're heading out to Wilkin's Mine."

"We managed to find a very small bit of mineral, orickite, on Drake Nobles's body. It was an odd find and the first bit of evidence, aside from those damn little nursery-rhyme words from 'Pop Goes the Weasel', that we've managed to get. Oddly enough, orickite is only found in this area."

"So are you thinking the killer is a geologist or a miner?"

"I'm not thinking anything. I'm just following evidence. I want to see the mine, poke around, talk to the owner and then see what shakes out."

"You know the owner might not want to chat. He's not what you'd call friendly."

"You know him?"

He shrugged. "I wouldn't say I know him, per se, but I know *of* him. I know enough to say I think being down in that mine has pickled his brain a little."

"Is he dangerous?"

"I guess we'll see."

"Have you had run-ins with him before?"

"A time or two. Nothing serious. He's a crazy old coot, but basically harmless. As long as you don't try to take his pot. Then, we might have a problem."

"Great. Another pot grower. You might want to remind people there's a law against that."

"Not since Prop 215. Gotta love those liberal California voters. As long as you've got a medical card, not much the law around here is going to do about it. I don't have the resources to chase after every illegal grower. My superiors have a 'don't ask, don't tell' policy. You know how it is around here. Nothing much has changed. Besides, they're harmless. They grow their weed and if they're left alone, they leave everyone else alone."

"It's still against the law," she said stiffly.

"Yeah. But I've learned to pick my battles."

She met his gaze briefly and looked away, unable to stare too long without fear of falling into those blue eyes and drowning. "I suppose you have a point, but it's still not right," she added.

They rode in silence, letting the music fill the car instead of their chatter—not that she could've mustered anything resembling frivolous chatter, her nerves were so taut. She had just managed to allow her mind to settle down when Matthew deliberately seemed to poke at a tender spot.

"Why didn't you come to the funeral?" he asked in a deceptively casual voice, as if that question wasn't charged with emotional pitfalls. When she didn't answer right away,

he said, "Your name was the last word he ever spoke. Did
you know that?"

"No."

"Of course you didn't. You weren't around."

"Don't do this."

"Don't do what? Talk about the past? Why not? We've
got a lot of history. Nothing wrong with reminiscing."

"You're not reminiscing. You're dredging up old crap.
When did you turn into such a passive-aggressive prick,
Matthew? If you've got something to say to me, get it out.
Say it. Say it or shove it up your ass because I don't answer
to you. I never did and I never will."

"You need to work on your people skills."

She shot him a look. "And you need to work on professional civility."

He drew himself up and then sighed, surprising her
with his agreement. "You're not the first person to tell me
that. But then, Neal was always the talker. The one who
could smooth everything out and make you wonder what
the hell you were mad about in the first place."

True. A vision of Neal as she liked to remember him
came back to soften the tense muscles in her mouth. He
was grinning like the devil, that ridiculously adorable
dimple of his flashing as he threw his head back and
laughed at something they'd said in their long-ago past.
"Yeah, he was quite the charmer when he wanted to be,"
she admitted. She had a treasure trove of memories to draw
from. She remembered how her heart had broken when she
realized Briana was not Neal's. She couldn't even pretend.
Whereas Neal had been fair-haired and looked the part
of the beautiful beach bum, Matthew had always looked
the part of…law enforcement. She stifled an inappropriate
urge to giggle. Matthew couldn't look like a bum if he
tried. Neal had been adept at making lounging look like

art; Matthew had been adept at making lounging look like hard work. A smile born of sweet memories tilted the corners of her mouth until she remembered that Neal was gone. The smile faded and she swallowed the lump in her throat. "I heard his parents moved away," she said, feeling as if she were listening to the conversation from elsewhere.

"Losing Neal…it was too hard for them."

She could imagine. Neal had been an only child. She shuddered to think of how bereft she'd feel if anything happened to Briana. "I loved them. They treated me like family," she murmured, feeling that awful twinge of guilt again. She'd wanted to go to the funeral, desperately, but she'd just found out she was pregnant and couldn't hold a cracker down, she was so sick. If she'd shown up, barfing her guts up every two seconds throughout the ceremony, it wouldn't have been hard to put the pieces together. Only everyone would've assumed the baby was Neal's, and even then she had an inkling it could be Matthew's. And boy, would that truth have been a barn-burner. She couldn't do that to Neal's parents.

She could feel Matthew judging her again. His silence said volumes. Her mouth itched to admit that she'd wanted to come but she couldn't very well tell him why she'd spent that day bawling her heart out on her secondhand sofa, crying so hard her body ached from the pain twisting her in half instead of being here, where she'd belonged, weeping alongside those who had also loved Neal.

"I couldn't get away," she said, the words strangling her, yet she kept her gaze locked on the scenery. "I was new to the bureau. I couldn't just leave on such short notice."

She caught his dark look. *Total bullshit,* that's what it said. Who was she to argue? She didn't even try. Instead, she turned the heat on him. "Who'd you end up marrying?"

"You don't know her."

"So she wasn't from around here?"

"No."

"How'd you meet?"

He shot an assessing look her way. "You really want to know?"

She shrugged. "Why not?"

Matthew slowed to take a tight ten-mile-an-hour switch-back, answering as the road straightened out. "We met at a bar in Fort Bragg. She was singing in a band called Phoenix Landing. She had a way about her that just forced you to pay attention. I couldn't take my eyes off her. Just like everyone else in the bar. But for whatever reasons, she and I hit it off. We were married within three months and divorced after five years."

"Let me guess…she didn't take very well to the isolated small-town bit."

"Good guess. Mari was…free-spirited. In the end, it was better to say goodbye than try to hold on to something that died a long time ago. She went back to singing in her band and I haven't seen her since."

"You sound like you've handled it well," she observed, curious if the calm face was an act. Matthew had always been good at poker. "I mean…you don't sound all broken up about it."

"My marriage ended. It wasn't my finest moment. I loved her. I wanted to build a life with her."

The last statement stung for a reason Kara wasn't comfortable examining any further. "I'm sorry it didn't work out," she murmured, needing to say something in the face of that quiet admission.

He shifted minutely, as if her condolences didn't sit

well with him and the moment returned to its previous awkwardness. Her sentiment hung between them until Kara wished she'd remained silent.

The girl, head aching from the stuff that had knocked her out, twisted in the tight bonds that lashed her feet and hands together. She clamped down on the nasty-tasting gag to keep from whimpering when the rope bit into her wrists. She could hear a television in another room of the house, the volume suddenly getting louder, until it was no trouble at all making out the newscast.

They were talking about a missing girl. Her hopes rose. Were they looking for her? She strained to pick out the details. Just as suddenly as her hope took flight, it crashed to the ground when she realized they weren't looking for her, but some other little girl. Someone named Hannah. She squeezed back tears of fear and shifted in her bonds. The urge to pee intensified until her bladder ached. Would this person make her pee in her pants? She swallowed against the gag. Fresh tears rolled down her cheeks.

She wanted her mommy. "Please find me," she whispered against the bond, her tongue automatically pushing against the wet rag until she made herself gag. "Hurry, please."

Chapter 6

Matthew cursed himself for sharing personal—painfully personal—information with Kara. It just sort of slipped out and that was out of character for him. His grip tightened on the steering wheel as he concentrated on the road. But a quick glance at Kara told him she was squirming under the weight of the moment, too. It had been frighteningly easy to fall into old habits, lulled by the phantom of their long-dead friendship, to let that bit of information out, and Matthew didn't like it.

But there was something about Kara that pulled at him. She had that enigmatic quality that so few have that drew a person to her. Much like Mari. Except Mari's charismatic energy had needed the stage to come alive. Kara was the opposite. She worked actively to downplay that magic. He could tell from the news conference footage he'd downloaded from the Net the night Kara arrived. He'd told himself he was watching to get more acquainted with the case but he'd really wanted to see how much Kara had changed, or if she'd remained the same. Physically, she was the woman he remembered. The woman made a man's teeth ache for want of something to bite. She had that sultry, secret and intense focus that reflected from her steady, unfaltering stare but there was a guardedness that hadn't been there before. What had happened to put that there? She hadn't been very forthcoming about anything personal in her own life, that much he noticed. And something had her on edge. She said it was the case. Certainly plausible. This case was giving him problems, too. Kara knew things like this just didn't happen in Lantern Cove. To call the small inland town *sleepy* would be like calling the pope mildly religious. And he liked it that way.

"I've seen your previous press conferences. You want me to do the honors this time around or are you going to do it?" he asked.

She seemed relieved, if not troubled by the topic, to break the silence with something they could talk about safely. "As much as I would relish handing that hellish detail off to someone else, I'll do it. I figure it won't be long before the press hears about Hannah Linney's body. The next of kin was contacted last night. It won't be long before you've got reporters crawling all over this place."

"If they can find it," Matthew said, only half joking. Lantern Cove was the only town on the Lost Coast not connected by Highway 1 or 101. It was as if the Cove's forefathers didn't much care about being connected to the rest of the world. And sometimes it still felt that way.

"Don't let the geography give you a false sense of security," Kara warned derisively. "When the press get a hold of something, they turn into bloodhounds. They'll be here. If they're not already. Trust me."

Great. Just what he needed to deal with, a bunch of nosy

reporters, asking questions and making a general nuisance of themselves for the sake of a thirty-second news clip.

Kara looked troubled. "I really want to have more to go with than what I've been saying already. The press are having a field day with this and I'd rather not feed the two-headed media beast without something to whet its appetite."

"You don't think the news that another child has been found is juicy enough to keep them chewing on that bone for a few more days?"

"Oh, it's juicy enough. That's the problem. It's too easy to sensationalize the tragedy. That's what I don't want. The killer is out there, no doubt watching just like everyone else, loving the attention. I don't want to feed that bastard's lust for pain."

For just a moment Matthew caught sight of the woman he used to know, compassionate and dedicated to the cause of justice, and he had to remind himself to pull back.

"Why were you chosen to be the mouthpiece for the Babysitter cases?" he asked, curiosity winning out. He knew Kara didn't enjoy the spotlight.

Her mouth tightened. "All the wrong reasons."

"What do you mean?"

She shook her head, obviously not wanting to go further. It only made him need to know more. "So it wasn't your experience level?"

"That would've been the right reason," she answered, huffing a short breath before looking at him to answer bluntly. "My face."

His confusion was clear. "Come again?"

"My director wanted me on the case because I have a nice enough face—*pretty*." She nearly spat the word, making it sound like a bad thing. "Because he believes the bureau could use some softening up in the eyes of the press. It's stupid, I know. But not much I could do about it. The fact is, I am the most qualified to handle the press on this case but I hate that my director didn't think of that as the reason. It's like thirty years of feminist advances never existed."

"So what you're saying is your director is a sexist idiot."

She risked a small smile. "I guess I am."

"Well, that may be true but I've watched your footage and you handle it well. I think you're the right person for the job. If my opinion counts for anything," he added as an afterthought.

A part of him hoped to see that tiny twitch of her lips turn into a full-fledged grin like old times, but she smothered it and returned to watching the scenery.

Matthew followed her lead, feeling like an idiot for even wandering into such territory with her. It was dangerous. If he started to think of her as a friend, the lines he drew in the sand might blur. Ten years was a long time to nurse a wound, he knew that. But after what she did to Neal, what they both did, if he couldn't forgive himself, he sure as hell couldn't forgive her, either.

That left them both in a very lonely place.

And he sure as hell already knew that. Something told him, so did she.

Dillon walked to the place called Tally's at the Pier and wrinkled his nose at the fishy smell of the waterfront that not even the heavy aroma from the fried food could smother. He'd never been one for the ocean. He pushed open the narrow door and went inside the dimly lit diner. The only light came from the porthole-type windows facing the ocean, which were designed to make tourists feel as if they really were aboard some kind of fishing boat. It just made him feel claustrophobic.

Openly suspicious stares came his way from the crusty locals seated at the bar, and he flashed a disarming grin their way that was not returned in the least. So much for making friends, he thought as he moved toward a man who looked as if he might be the owner.

With wild, white hair standing on end as if electrified, he stood wiping down beer steins behind the bar, noting the moment Dillon walked into the establishment.

As Dillon approached, the man gestured. "You one of those FBI guys?" he asked.

Dillon flashed his badge. "That obvious, huh? Are you Tally by any chance?"

The man raised an eyebrow made of stiff white hairs long enough to curl. "No. Tally was my pops. I'm Chuck." He lifted a stein. "How about a beer? I know how you Brits love your beer. I have Guinness and Newcastle."

"Tempting, but I just had breakfast and unfortunately, loaded up on orange juice," Dillon joked, but the humor fell flat and died a quiet death as Chuck just gave him a fish-eyed stare that would've make Groucho Marx pack up and go home. "Right. On second thought, a beer sounds just the thing. Whatever you have on draft."

Chuck took the stein in his hand and filled it up.

Wiping away the foam, he smiled. "Perfect. Nothing like a cold brew before 10:00 a.m. Invigorating."

Chuck seemed to loosen up. Leaning against the bar, he flicked at a lone peanut and it skittered across the floor. "Sad news about that kid," he said. "What a sicko bastard."

It was one of those leading statements that people often used to draw someone else into a conversation. Dillon was happy to oblige. He was there for information. Besides, by all appearances, Chuck seemed the kind of guy who noticed things—or people—that didn't belong.

"Yeah, that's for sure," Dillon agreed amicably, taking another draught, not even the least bit concerned that he was indulging while on the clock. "What can you tell me about the area of Wolf's Tooth? Is it popular with the locals?"

"Only the ones who know what they're doing. It's not exactly tourist friendly and you sure as hell ain't gonna find it on no hiking map. Too many steep inclines. That's why it's called that. One false move and you're falling to your death. The ferns and bracken hide how sharp of a drop the ravine actually is."

That's what he figured. "So it's only big with the locals?"

"Only the ones with a death wish or the ones who have something to hide."

Pot growers, perhaps? Dillon wisely kept that observation to himself. Seeing as this was the only joint in town that served alcohol, Dillon asked, "Have you noticed anyone different coming in lately? Someone other than the locals?"

"Not this time of year," Chuck said, grabbing another stein to dry with his less-than-pristine white towel. Dillon tried not to think of that and just hoped Chuck didn't also use that towel to wipe his nose...or other places. "Tourist season—such as it is—is over. Now it's just the locals coming in."

"Is there anyone you think I might want to talk to?" he asked.

Chuck looked at him as if he'd grown another head, then shook his own. "Nope."

Dumb question. Locals stick together in places like this. Loyalty ran thicker than blood. Knowing he wouldn't get any further with this guy, Dillon finished his beer and then headed out.

He walked the tiny row of shops, digesting the ale and the information he'd gotten from Chuck. Was it possible the person they were looking for was local to Lantern Cove? It seemed an impossibly convenient break in the case, which immediately made the possibility suspect in his mind. Nothing was that simple. The obvious answer was not always the right one, especially when they were dealing with psychos like the Babysitter.

But he'd stupid to overlook the possibility just the same. Pulling out his BlackBerry, he sent a group text to the CARD Team with the information he'd gleaned and headed for a shop that advertised maps of the area. He wanted to get to know Wolf's Tooth just a little better. The topography, the history. He didn't want to jump to conclusions but his intuition—not that he believed in that nonsense—was telling him to dig a little deeper. And he was happy to do so.

He spared a moment's thought wondering how Kara was faring with the local lawman, and a rare, genuine smile lit his face. He wasn't in a habit of screwing with his partner but he had to admit watching Kara around the man—*tense* was the word—was entertaining. What a complete bastard of him, he knew. But he never pretended to be a saint. Not even close.

He was just stepping into the store, the scent of old building assaulting his senses, but before he could raise a mocking brow at the tourist-heavy fare of T-shirts and coffee mugs, he answered his phone without thinking. Director Colfax's voice came across the line and he grimaced. Colfax was a right bastard and Dillon usually let Kara deal with him.

"Where's Kara?" Colfax asked in a quiet voice that was

so unlike the blustery blowhard. His tone immediately put Dillon on alert. "She's not answering her cell."

"She's no doubt out of range. She went up to a place called Wilkin's Mine to follow up on that mineral lead. Why?"

The heavy silence on the other end sent a wave of foreboding rolling across Dillon's skin. "Why? What's wrong?" he asked, his stomach muscles constricting for no good reason.

"We have a situation. It's personal. Find her, McIntyre. Immediately."

Colfax was an asshole but he wasn't prone to melo-dramatics. Something bad was in the air. Dillon could feel it as strongly as the cold, foggy air biting through his jacket.

Shit. He did an about-face and bolted to his car.

Chapter 7

Kara trudged up the narrow driveway behind Matthew to the shack masquerading as a house owned by Bernal Poff, also the licensed owner of Wilkin's Mine.

"So what does he mine for?" Kara asked, a little out of breath after the sharp hike from the road to the house. The misty air permeated her lungs and made each draw feel like icicles were forming. She was accustomed to the Bay Area damp but she'd forgotten how much colder the northern coast was in comparison. "Gold or something?"

Matthew smirked. "Or something. Treasure."

She did a double take. "Excuse me?"

"Bernie Poff has spent most of his adult life looking for a treasure that was supposedly buried in Lantern Cove in the late 1800s by an old Indian trader. He bought Wilkin's Mine when he discovered the old tunnel that supposedly fit the description of the one that concealed the lost treasure."

"Oh, c'mon," Kara said in annoyance. "You're kidding me, right? People don't waste their lives on treasure hunts anymore. That's ridiculous."

He shrugged. "I'm not arguing. Just stating the facts as I know them," he said, going to the door and giving it a solid knock. He gestured for her to be silent and play along. Before she could scowl, he explained in a rush, "Bernie's not a people person and seems to have a real sour spot for women. So, just let me do the talking this time around."

She snapped her mouth shut and tried not to let her ears steam. This was an excellent example of why she'd moved away from this backward place. "Fine," she stated tersely but it made her teeth ache just to say it. "Make sure you ask him if we can go up to the mine."

He had just enough time to nod when the door cracked open a slit. Matthew stepped back so Bernie could get a good look at him.

"What you wantin'? I ain't done nothin' wrong," Bernie said from behind the door. "Git off my property unless you got a warrant, lawman."

"We're just here to talk, Bernie. C'mon, now, open the door and let's talk like gentlemen."

Kara slanted an amused look Matthew's way in spite of her previous annoyance. She'd never seen Matthew cajole anyone before with such a nice way about him. Smooth as silk. She had no idea he had that kind of talent. Seems a bit of Neal had rubbed off after all.

The door opened a bit wider and Kara stiffened when Bernie's dour expression soured even more when he saw her. "Who's she?" he demanded.

Screw this nice routine. She had a job to do. Stepping forward, she said, "I'm Special Agent Kara Thistle with the FBI. May we have a few words with you, Mr. Poff?"

"I hate the damn feds! Git off my damn property!" And

the door slammed shut. From behind the door, they heard him ranting about the "freedom-stealing sons-of-bitches" and then something about the right to bear arms.

Matthew's mouth tightened and he gave her a warning look that she felt guilty enough to deserve for some stupid reason. But she wasn't about to let one asshole recluse get the best of her. She looked at Matthew and pounded on the door. "Now we do things my way," she said with a sweet smile.

"Be my guest."

"Bernal Poff, open this door or I will have it torn off the hinges. You are impeding a federal investigation and if you don't want more feds crawling all over your property, I suggest you open this damn door. Now!"

Silence answered her request. Matthew wore a smirk. "That worked wonders," he said. "Yet it seems we're no closer than when we started. He's not going to open that door."

"Yes, he will," Kara said from between gritted teeth. Damn the man for being right. "Open the door, you old fart."

The last part was muttered but Matthew chuckled. "Standard operating procedure, calling people old farts?"

"I call it as I see it," she said, irritation for being stonewalled by some crazy idiot sharpening her voice. "So you think you have something better in mind?" she asked in exasperation.

"I did and I was doing it until you went all G.I. Jane."

"That's the navy."

"Whatever. Step aside."

Kara speared him with a dark look but was willing to let him try. She wasn't lying about having this place crawl with feds but it would take a few hours to get them here and she didn't feel like waiting that long to get a few answers to her questions.

Matthew knocked again. "Bernie...c'mon, now. There's no reason to act like this. We just want to ask a few questions. My colleague apologizes if she seemed rude."

"I do not apologize," Kara whispered. "That's a flat-out lie, Matthew Keenan Beauchamp. I wasn't rude."

"Shh," he said from the corner of his mouth.

She buttoned her lip but kept a mutinous expression. She was just about to tell Matthew to forget it, she'd get reinforcements and toss the old coot on his ear, when the door opened a crack.

"Just you," Bernie instructed, pointing a stubbed and grubby finger at Matthew. "I don't cotton to listenin' to some FBI broad yammer at me. What do you want?"

"Fine, Bernie. Open the door a bit, please," Matthew said.

The door swung wider and Bernie Poff, a short, squat and permanently stunted man stepped into view. Years of traveling the labyrinth of tunnels under the mountain had given him the appearance of a troll. There was no nicer way to describe the man standing at the door. She could see dirt wedged under his nails and she doubted he had seen a bar of soap since the '80s. If one were to go by appearances, this guy could fit the stereotypical bill for a bad guy—if they were living in a Grimms fairy tale.

"So state yur business," Bernie demanded, giving Kara a dark look before skewing his gaze back to Matthew. "I ain't got all day."

"A geologist tracked a very rare mineral to your mine, or at least one in the very near vicinity, and we need to ask you some questions."

"Why fer?"

"The mineral was found at a crime scene. You familiar with the Babysitter case?"

Bernie grunted an affirmative and his expression softened just a bit. "Seen it on the news," he admitted. "Someone ain't right in the head to do that to kids. Is this about those cases?"

Matthew nodded. "That's why it's important you co-operate. We're not here to bother you about anything else."

Bernie eyed Matthew with open suspicion but something else had entered the light of his stare, as well. Kara couldn't readily identify it but it seemed similar to…fear. That struck an odd note.

"Fine. What do you want to know?"

"Has anyone else, aside from you, been in the mine lately?" Matthew asked.

"Hell no. I don't run a timeshare. This is my land and I keep everyone else off it." His voice had taken on a possessive—almost paranoid—tone, and Kara's stare narrowed speculatively. "And I'd know if someone were up there. I've got the whole place booby-trapped."

Kara's gaze widened but she held her tongue. She didn't want the old man to stop talking.

"All right. I believe you. But my colleague needs to take some samples from the mine. Can you take us up there to do that?"

Kara held up a small plastic evidence canister. Bernie eyed the canister with suspicion. "Just a sample? You don't have to go into the mine, right?"

Kara couldn't resist. "Is there some reason you don't want us in the mine, Mr. Poff?"

"Cuz it's mine," Bernie snapped.

She shot Matthew a look. If the samples matched, that meant whoever had killed the Nobles boy had been tromping around in Bernie Poff's mine for whatever reasons. But she supposed they'd cross that bridge later... when they had more people with guns.

Matthew and Kara were back in the car and heading back down the mountain when Kara tried to access her voice mail.

"Damn. The service here sucks," she said, holding her phone up to see that she had no reception. "How far until we get service?"

"We've got to get out of the trees first. Probably when we hit the highway again. Why?"

"I have to check in with the team. We rarely go this long without radio contact. Dillon is probably calling me all sorts of names in that British accent of his."

Matthew kept his face neutral but the urge to say something unflattering about her pretty-boy partner was strong. It wasn't just that Brit-boy was too good-looking to be taken seriously, it was that he knew Kara as she was now, whereas Matthew only had memories. And why should that bother him? Hell, he didn't want to dig into that bucket of chum. He just knew that the Brit rubbed him the wrong way and every time Matthew saw him, he wanted to put his fist through his pretty face.

"So...you two an item or anything?" he asked. The question was casual but the feelings squeezing his chest weren't. Why should he care even if they were? He almost rescinded the question but Kara answered before he could.

"Dillon? He's my partner and he's become a friend but no, there's nothing between us. Never has and never will. He's not my type."

That simple admission made whatever was squeezing his chest loosen, which was a good thing, but at the same time it seemed to scale back the controls on his mouth, which was not a good thing.

He cocked his head as he contemplated her answer. "So, was there another Neal for you out there?"

Kara seemed to stiffen and he knew he'd struck a tender nerve. He hadn't meant to...but maybe he had. Who knows? His feelings were always a jumbled mess when it came to Kara.

"Why do you think it would be so easy to forget Neal?" she asked quietly, the barely cloaked echo of her anguish shocking him. "I loved him. He was my world. When he left it, a part of me died with him. But that's hard for you to believe, isn't it? Because I didn't go to the funeral?"

Her quiet accusation hit home and he answered with honesty. "There are other reasons."

Kara looked away but not before he caught the shame in her eyes. "Yeah. I live with that guilt every day. You have no idea."

Matthew remained silent. Confessions of a dangerous sort filled his mouth but prudence kept them from spilling. Instead, he just backed out of the conversation with a terse apology. "Forget what I said. The past is dead. I shouldn't have said anything."

Kara gave him an odd look—like a scared, trapped rabbit's—but jerked her head in agreement. "Thanks," she whispered.

"Don't mention it."

They rode in excruciating silence all the way back to the motel. Matthew didn't know what was worse, the tense quiet or the dialogue running through his head, berating him for being a sanctimonious prick all too eager to crucify Kara not only for her sins but for his own, as well. God, he'd nursed that anger against Kara for so long it burned bright and hot with just the smallest breath of air to fan it alive again, but he sensed a sadness in her that threw him off. He'd never imagined that perhaps Kara had been hurting, too. And that stung worse than anything else. He'd been too wrapped up in his own pain and guilt to consider what Kara had been going through. Perhaps it was time to let bygones be bygones....

He turned to Kara, ready to make amends and try to repair their tattered, yet joined, past, but the bloodless expression on Kara's face as she held her cell phone to her ear sent a terrifying zing straight to his gut.

"Kara? What's wrong?" he demanded, irrational fear buzzing in his ear for no reason other than the way Kara's hand was shaking. "Kara? Talk to me!"

When she looked at him, she whispered in a strangled cry, "Oh God, drive faster."

Chapter 8

Kara's fingers were numb from twisting her hands into knots as Matthew drove as fast as he could without putting them over the edge of a cliff.

Matthew had given up trying to pry out of her what was wrong. It wouldn't have mattered. Her vocal cords were paralyzed. Fear slithered in and around her heart, squeezing until she couldn't breathe. This couldn't be happening. Not to her.

Matthew threw the Jeep into Park and she bolted from the vehicle. She nearly collided with Dillon. He gripped her arms tightly and stared into her eyes.

"We will find her," he promised.

She jerked a nod, but how many times had she uttered those same words to terrified parents only to know in her heart the chances were slim that their child would come home safely if they didn't find them within forty-eight hours.

"What's going on?" Matthew asked, staring her down, demanding an answer. Her mouth worked but tears rushed to the surface. Dillon answered for her. His voice grave.

"We think the Babysitter has taken Briana."

"Who is Briana?" he asked.

Dillon caught the minute shake of Kara's head but chose to ignore it. "Kara's daughter."

She felt rather than saw Matthew's shock and when she turned to slowly meet his gaze, the stark expression in his stare confirmed it. "How old?"

Swallowing, she looked away before answering, not wanting to see what would flash in his eyes at her response. "Nine."

Clinging to her professional training, she pushed Matthew out of her head and tried not to key in on the panic twisting her thought process. To save Briana, she had to keep her head on straight. Instead, she turned to Dillon and said, "Tell me everything you know."

Matthew's knees locked as an automatic response the moment he felt his leg muscles weaken. It felt as if he'd just taken a roundhouse kick to the sternum yet nothing had touched him. Kara avoided looking him in the eye. He could attribute that to the situation, but he was fairly certain guilt had something to do with it, as well.

A daughter. Kara had a daughter. The night they shared broke free from his cache of memories and slammed into the mental theater of his mind, obliterating everything else. Her skin, bathed in moonlight, the surf crashing against the rock, the smell of the sea mingling with that of Kara's personal scent and the overwhelming guilt they both shared afterward. It was all imprinted—no, branded—into his memory. Was it possible they had created a child that night? His mind balked. No. It had to be Neal's baby. But he couldn't deny there was a possibility…and that child was in danger.

"The housekeeper found Mai. Her throat was cut," Dillon began. Kara's eyes watered but she remained silent so Dillon wouldn't stop. Matthew felt the grief coming off her in waves and he wondered who Mai was to her. He assumed it was the child's nanny. "No sign of a struggle. It looks as if the perp snuck up from behind. She probably never knew what hit her and died almost instantly."

"And Briana?" Kara could barely get the words out. "What of Briana?"

"The housekeeper searched the house but there was no sign of her."

"What makes you think it's the Babysitter?" Matthew interjected.

Dillon paused, his countenance grim. "It's the first time he's left something behind that wasn't hidden. A note. *Come chase the weasel.*"

"The bastard is taunting us. I told you he was spelling out the words to that cursed nursery rhyme with his previous victims," Kara said, disgust curling her lip. Her voice lowered to a harsh whisper. "When we catch him…I'm going to kill him."

Suddenly Dillon looked uncomfortable, causing Kara to look at him sharply. "What? Why are you giving me that look?"

"Kara, this is hard to tell you but you can't be on the case any longer. As evidenced by that comment, you've lost your objectivity. Colfax pulled you off, effective immediately."

Kara exploded. "Like hell I am. My daughter is out there with a maniac and you think I'm just going to go home and twiddle my thumbs while hoping for the best? I think you know what my answer to that is, so let's stop wasting time and find this bastard before—" she swallowed and blinked back a wash of tears "—before…before…oh, shit…we just have to find him."

Dillon's face pulled into a concerned frown but he shook his head just the same. "Kara…you're a liability to the investigation now, you know that! How many parents have we had to deal with under similar circumstances? More than we would like, and a frantic, grief-stricken parent isn't going to be helpful. As hard as it is, trust in us that we will do everything in our power to find Briana. *Trust us.*"

Kara's mouth worked but no words came out. Matthew sensed a breakdown was coming and he knew Kara was not the type to blubber like a baby in the company of others. When she cried, she chose to do it in the shower, where no one could see her. He knew this simply because when growing up, Kara had often run to Matthew's house when her pop had gotten out of hand and smacked her around a bit.

"Let's take a walk," he suggested, his voice carefully neutral. "Take a breather."

Dillon nodded. "I'll call if I hear anything."

Kara looked rooted to the spot until Matthew tugged at her hand. She went reluctantly, as if her feet were dragging in molasses, but the important thing was that she went. The fight left her and she followed Matthew.

They walked to her motel room and Kara let them in woodenly. She tossed the key to the table and sat on the edge of the bed. Suddenly, she dropped her head in her hands. He expected to hear sobs but she held the tears inside. So like Kara. He sat beside her. "Do you need to take a shower?" he asked.

She glanced at him through a curtain of hair before she pushed a lock behind her ears. Mossy green eyes glazed with pain stared back at him. Her throat worked as she tried swallowing and she finally nodded. "Yeah," she croaked, and even though he wanted answers he knew she needed time to put herself back together again. He'd give her that.

"Go shower. Then we'll talk."

It wasn't an invitation for chitchat. Matthew knew Kara understood when she gave him a short, curt nod before rising stiffly and closing herself into the small bathroom.

Matthew used the time to check in with the station. In very short detail, he gave Oren the newest information. He skipped the part where the child that was missing could be his or Neal's. He figured there was no sense in sharing that detail just yet until he had the facts.

Hanging up the phone, he noticed a small picture frame beside the bedside lamp. He picked it up. His heart stopped.

A miniature version of himself smiled back at him.

Kara exited the bathroom, wrapped in her robe, a towel twisted on top of her head, just in time to see Matthew pick up the photo beside her bed. She'd always wondered what would happen if this moment came and she figured she'd probably lie. But when Matthew's stark gaze met hers, she couldn't bring herself to utter a word that wasn't truthful. Besides, the effort would've been futile. Matthew knew the truth. It was staring right at him with a gap-toothed grin and ocean-blue eyes.

"She's mine."

"Yes."

He continued to stare at the photo as if memorizing every detail. If it weren't for the fact that their daughter was missing, she would've suffocated under the weight of her own guilt, but as it was she was simply resigned to whatever would happen between them. She deserved his anger, his grief, whatever he was feeling. She'd denied him knowledge of his flesh and blood. She felt lower than low but she couldn't deal with that right now.

Instead, she tried explaining her decision as if he weren't the father of her lost child but rather just another colleague and she was going over a case file. She needed that detachment right now.

"I found out I was pregnant a month after I left. I'd just started with the FBI and was overwhelmed. I made the wrong choice. I realize that now. But I didn't know if the baby was yours or Neal's." She met his gaze without flinching. "I'd prayed she was Neal's but the moment I saw her, I knew. And there was no way I could come back here and tell you that we'd created a child. Neal's death was still so new and the pain was so sharp. I knew you'd want Briana to be here in Lantern Cove, close to you and your family, and I didn't think I could handle dealing with people's reactions. Particularly Neal's parents. They would've been crushed. It seemed best to just stay away. I never figured we'd meet up again or that you'd ever find out about Briana."

His expression darkened and she had to look away. Still, even though she wasn't looking at him, she could feel the chill coming from him.

"How could you keep my daughter from me?"

"I just told you why," Kara answered sharply. "I don't need you to tell me I made a selfish choice but it seemed the best at the time. I was young, scared and grieving. But I had a career to cling to. Briana and the job was all I had."

"If I'd known, I would've been there for my child," he said.

"I know that. All I can say is I'm sorry."

"And if that's not good enough?"

"It has to be. Our daughter is missing. Let's just find her. We'll figure everything out later."

Kara held her breath. She was asking a lot, but damn it, it's not like they had many options. She'd gladly sit through anything Matthew wanted to dish out later but right now, she could give a flying shit about his hurt feelings. She needed to focus on getting Briana home safely. Her stomach tightened as an image of Hannah's body rolled through her mind, except this time it was her own daughter's body and she nearly lost the strength in her legs. "I'm sorry," she whispered, genuinely apologetic, but the hard glint in Matthew's eyes didn't soften.

"All right. We'll do things your way. For now," he bit out, and Kara fought the urge to wince. "We'd better find her. Thanks to you I could lose my daughter before I ever get the chance to know her. What you've done is unforgivable. When this is all over, things are going to change. That's a promise."

No. It was a threat. That's how Kara perceived his statement and she couldn't help but bristle.

"What's that supposed to mean?"

"You're a smart woman. Figure it out." Matthew didn't give her a chance for a rebuttal. He spun on his booted heel and stalked from the room. She could practically see the steam coming from the tops of his ears. A cool-off was probably wise. Neither one of them needed to let emotions cloud their judgment.

Her hands shaking, she drew the picture frame from the table and cupped it to her breast. A single tear snaked its way down her cheek, proving she hadn't expended all her tears in the shower. Her baby. Was she hurt? The Babysitter kept the victims tied and bound until he suffocated them with something. Fibers gathered from the Nobles boy's nostril indicated his killer had probably used a pillow. But no fibers were collected from the other two victims. The damnable lump rose in her throat again and she gagged it down. Her baby was not going to die.

Chapter 9

Matthew's spinning thoughts warred with his need to focus but it was easier said than done when your world had splintered apart.

He had a child. *Briana*. He tested her name on his tongue and he choked up. All this time lost. Fury tangled with the anguish over the situation and he didn't know how to process how he was feeling. His hands curled with the need to break something, needing that outlet to vent the violence twisting his heart into something black and ugly.

The hatred he'd nursed against Kara for what she'd done to Neal paled in comparison to what he was feeling at that moment against the mother of his child. *Mother of his child*. That startling thought sobered him like a slap in the face. No longer just a childhood friend or ex-fiancée of his best friend. No longer the woman of his secret

dreams. They were tied together in the most unbreakable
way—DNA.

He expelled a long breath and watched as it curled and
dissipated into the frosty air. His gaze traveled the treetops
set against the gray sky and he sent a silent prayer that they
found Briana before it was too late.

Dillon regarded the silent group before him. They were
all feeling the same thing. Shock. They all knew Briana,
loved her like their own. The kid was easy to like. Smart
without being precocious, cute that bordered on beautiful,
which meant when she grew up...Dillon looked away. They
had to ensure she had a chance to grow up and break
hearts.

"This ain't right," D'Marcus muttered, tossing his pen
to the makeshift desk where his computer center was
situated. "Kara's part of the team. She's been a part since
the beginning. No one knows this case better than her. We
need her insight."

Dillon agreed but his hands were tied. "Colfax was
pretty clear. Kara could jeopardize the investigation at
this point."

"That's bullshit and you know it," Tana interjected with
a dark look. "If anyone could do this, it's Kara. She's not
like anyone else. Not like most parents. She can detach
and be the agent she needs to be."

Dillon shook his head. "It's her daughter and she's only
human."

"You know if we don't at least let her in on the sideline
she's going to go off and head the investigation herself.
Nothing is going to stop her. Not Colfax and not any stupid
rule that says she has to be off the case. She needs us and
we need her. What Colfax doesn't know won't hurt him,"
Tana said.

Dillon looked around the room, reading each expression, knowing they were waiting for him to fall into line. It wasn't that he didn't want Kara on the team and certainly not because he enjoyed toeing the line Colfax was giving him. He didn't want to do anything that would put Briana in more danger. Was Kara a loose cannon who would do more harm than good? Or would she continue to be the steady hand at the helm that they all—that Briana—needed?

Well, he knew Tana was right. Kara wouldn't sit like a good girl waiting for news of the investigation. She'd give the bureau the middle finger and head off on her own. They might as well give her the backup she'd need. "Fine. We're in agreement. Kara is in—but if anyone breathes a word about this, we're all in a heap of trouble. It's got to be total radio silence from here on out. I will deal with Colfax."

They all nodded and Dillon felt a weight fall from his shoulders. Colfax was a prat anyway. And Dillon rarely followed rules unless they suited him. Bad habit, that. Or so he'd been told. Repeatedly.

It was near to midnight when Kara finally tossed her reading glasses to the table and rubbed the grit from her eyes. A yawn jackknifed her mouth so hard her jaw popped but she didn't want to stop. The rest of the team had already dragged their bodies—stiff from sitting at the table poring over evidence and case files—to bed, but Kara knew she wouldn't find sleep even if she tried. She'd have to collapse first.

Raising her coffee cup, she took a tired swallow only to grimace at the ice-cold temperature. She considered heating it up, but considering it would do nothing for the flavor, she simply downed it, willing the caffeine to give her a second wind.

Dropping her head into the cradle of her arms, she closed her eyes for a moment. Cement dragged her eyelids but grief, purposefully buried, broke free and welled to the surface. She bit back the keening wail that threatened to burst from her throat but her nails dug into the flesh of her arms, the pain paling in comparison to the rending of her heart.

Would she see Briana again? What had been the last thing she'd said to her? Was it loving? Or was it tinged with exasperation as her voice sometimes tended to get when she was rushed and preoccupied with whatever was going on at work? She hoped not. She hoped the last words she spoke to Briana were ones that would serve to bolster her courage when she needed it the most.

Kara dragged a shuddering breath and released it forcefully, trying to stop the hysteria from gaining a foothold. She had to stay focused. She could do this. She *had* to do this.

But her brain, whether from extreme fatigue or grief, wouldn't cooperate so readily. Images from her memory flashed in slow succession, as bittersweet as they were treasured.

Briana slid into the world on a bone-bending push that Kara was sure was going to send the infant flying across the room from the force of it. Instead, she landed gracefully in the doctor's waiting hands, a small slippery bundle that would forever change Kara's life.

Kara had never known such love as she felt the moment she stared into those bright blue eyes and her daughter's infant fingers clutched instinctively around Kara's index finger.

And Kara had cried, feeling so alone. For a mad, crazy, hormonal moment she'd actually considered calling Matthew, but as her hand touched the phone, she jerked it back as if it had burned her. She couldn't tell him. It was at that moment she resolved to be a single parent.

And now…she swallowed with difficulty. Now her daughter was missing. If she hadn't been so selfish, Briana would've grown up here in Lantern Cove, safe from the lunatics that Kara chased every day, thriving.

Mai would still be alive.

Her fingers curled blindly, crumpling the paperwork beneath them. She didn't even notice. A sob rocked her body as the tears rolled unchecked down her cheek. There, at midnight with no one as her witness, she sobbed her heart out, wishing she could change that fateful decision. Rather than listening to her fears, she should have listened to her heart and dialed that phone on the day her daughter was born.

The phone rang and she jumped. Wiping at her eyes, she picked up on the second ring. It was Matthew.

"I knew you'd be awake."

She sniffed loudly, hoping Matthew wouldn't realize she'd been crying. "I don't sleep well under normal circumstances." She didn't need to say what they were both thinking. Somehow it seemed wrong to sleep when their daughter was missing, as if those hours spent snoozing might somehow jeopardize their chances of finding her. "How about you?"

"Same."

Silence followed until she heard him draw a deep breath. She felt the urge to apologize yet again but knew he hadn't called to hear her say how sorry she was. He knew. But it was likely he still hated her. Another tear snaked its way down her cheek. "Matthew—"

"What time should I be there tomorrow?" he asked, cutting her off brusquely.

"You don't need to be here," she started, then hesitated.

He did need to be there just as much as she did. "We start at 7:00 a.m."

"I'll be there." There was a long pause and Kara wondered why, when all there was left to say was goodbye. Then he asked in a tight, pained voice, "What is she like?"

Fresh tears sprang to her eyes and she struggled to keep the evidence from her voice. "She's a lot like you," she admitted. "She's a quiet kid, a watcher. She's smart, a straight-A student. Loves to learn. She just recently—" her voice caught on the words and when they finally did come out they were filled with a mother's anguish "—asked if she could take guitar lessons."

Matthew had started playing the guitar when they were eight, a year younger than Briana. His fingers hadn't quite been able to fret the strings properly but he'd been so proud of that guitar. It had startled Kara when Briana, out of the blue, asked if she could start taking lessons.

She heard him swallow and she knew he was pushing down tears, as well. This just sucked, she thought bitterly. Plain sucked all the way around.

"Did you buy her a guitar?"

"I was thinking about it. I—" She didn't want to admit that she'd been less than inclined to indulge Briana's wish. In fact, she'd suggested Briana take piano lessons instead, which hadn't gone over well with her daughter. "I will, though."

"Let me do it," he said.

Her first instinct was to decline his offer but the truth was out of the bag. What did it matter now? Besides, suddenly, Kara's priorities were different than they were days ago. Now, if she got Briana home safely, she'd let her play any instrument she damn well wanted to even if it did remind Kara how much she was like her father.

"All right," she agreed softly. "That would be nice."

He grunted something unintelligible and Kara sensed emotion was getting the best of him. She wasn't the only one who didn't enjoy letting others know how deeply something had touched her. He cleared his throat and said gruffly, "Tomorrow, then."

She nodded. "Yeah. Tomorrow."

All around the mulberry bush, the monkey chased the weasel…

A child's singsong voice drifted into her dreams and Kara tossed in her bed to get away from it.

The monkey thought 'twas all in fun, Pop! goes the weasel.

A sleepy groan escaped as the child's voice continued to sing. Shaking herself more fully awake, she expected the remnant of the odd dreamscape to fade but the song continued. Bolting upright, the hair on her arms standing at full attention, Kara gasped when the song abruptly stopped. She wasn't hearing things. A child had been singing to her. Flicking the light at her bedside, she blinked against the sudden illumination and felt sick to her stomach at the sight of an empty room. It was four in the morning. Same time as the last time something this creepy had happened.

Sagging against the pillow, she gave a shaky laugh. She was losing it.

Chapter 10

Matthew wasn't the first to notice that Kara looked like death warmed over, but he was the only one to comment on it. He received a nasty look that he probably deserved. He didn't want to care if she wasn't sleeping—or eating, judging by the look of her—but old habits die hard apparently.

"When's the last time you ate?" he asked.

She barely looked up from the geologist's report she was reading to answer distractedly, "Sometime yesterday I think. I had some almonds. Or maybe they were peanuts. I don't remember. Why?"

Matthew ignored the amused look the Brit shot him and stalked from the room. Ten minutes later he returned with fresh coffee—that stuff she'd been swilling had to be days old—and a Danish. He thrust it at her. "Best I can do on short notice. Eat," he commanded sternly. Her puzzled expression prompted him to explain. "Can't think with a fuzzy brain. You need food and sleep. Basic human functions."

Kara shot a quick look around at her team and then reluctantly took the Danish. "Thanks."

"Doesn't mean we're dating," Matthew said.

"A romantic," Dillon quipped, further cementing Matthew's distaste for the man. "Who knew? Got a Danish for me in that bag of tricks?"

"No."

Dillon grinned, not the least bit put out by Matthew's glower. "Good thing I brought my own breakfast, then."

"Good thing."

"Are you two finished?" Kara interrupted, annoyed. "You sound like two high school twits and it's giving me a headache. Are you ready to work or not?"

Dillon leaned conspiratorially toward Matthew and said in a whisper, "Look what we have to deal with when she hasn't had her coffee yet. We should get hazard pay."

Matthew almost smiled. "Got anything new?"

Kara's brows pulled into a faint frown as she answered reluctantly. "It's just a weird hunch…but I want to go over the details of each victim again. Something about that nursery rhyme is stuck in my head. There's got to be a clue we're missing."

"That's the whole point, isn't it?" Dillon said grimly. "The Babysitter wants to stump us. He thinks he's going to outsmart us."

"Right. And what kind of person has an ego like that?"

"A genius," Matthew put in, and Kara nodded.

"Exactly. I think we're looking for someone with an above-average intelligence and a superiority complex. Start compiling data on the universities with gifted programs in the cities where the vics were found. Something tells me our perp likes to be around people who also think they're smart just so he can show them up. This person has a sizable ego. He's going to want to show off just how smart he is."

"What makes you go there?" Dillon asked.

"The nursery rhyme itself. D'Marcus pulled some historical data on the rhyme, origin, meaning, things like that. I didn't think anything of it at first but as I reread the findings, I found that the rhyme has all these hidden meanings."

"Oh, goody, a history lesson," Dillon said, rolling his eyes. "Go on. I'm all ears."

"The rhyme goes all the way back to seventeenth-century England, then it eventually spread to the colonies. But it was a work song used by weavers using large loom racks."

"That makes perfect sense," Dillon interjected sourly. "I'm sure there's some kind of point coming?"

"Shut up and let her finish," Matthew said, interested in seeing where Kara was going with this. "Go on."

"*Monkey* and *weasel* were slang for the children they employed to sit inside these huge industrial loom machines and chase the loom shuttle around, unsticking it when it got off track and correcting any mis-weaves that happened as a result. The weavers started calling the kids 'monkeys' and 'weasels' because of all the hopping back and forth they did with their job and because they had to weave in and out of narrow passages between the racks like little weasels."

"A lot of kids died back then in the weaving factories," Matthew said, nodding. "Dark. Just like most nursery rhymes. Fitting. But how does that tie into the Babysitter?"

"I don't know," Kara admitted. "But I know there's

something there. That's why I want the team to research the universities for their gifted students. You know they say there's a fine line between genius and crazy. It's obvious our perp crossed the line between the two."

"I'll get D'Marcus trolling the university records and let you know if anything comes up. In the meantime, I'm going to see if Tana has those sample results you collected from the paranoid old man," Dillon said, and disappeared from the room.

"He's good, right?" Matthew asked, still eyeing the door where Dillon went out. "I mean, he's some kind of wunderkind, right?"

Kara's smile was brief and fatigued. "My entire team are experts in their field. And Dillon's no kid. He's our age. Good genes, I guess. Why?"

"I don't like him."

"Why not?" She looked puzzled.

"Maybe the accent. Maybe it's the fact he looks like Brad Pitt and talks like Hugh Grant." Matthew shrugged. "Maybe it's just because he got the chance to know my daughter when I didn't." Damn it, he hadn't meant to say that, but like Kara, he wasn't operating on much sleep and his mouth had gotten the better of him. Thankfully, he got a hold of his faculties before he let slip that he was torqued by the fact that it was obvious Dillon had slid into the spot that he should have occupied. As a mentor to Briana. And *that* above all else put him in a really foul mood. He told himself he could give a shit who Kara had in her life, but he resented that anyone but him could be close to his daughter. But now all that mattered was Briana. At least that much was true.

"She calls him Uncle Dillon," Kara acknowledged. "He's the closest thing to a father figure she's ever known even though Dillon's not what one would call conventionally father-figure-ish. Still, he's a good man. You should give him a chance."

"I have enough friends. I just want to find my daughter and once she's home, I will be her father."

"You've made your point, Matthew," Kara said, her back stiffening. "You don't need to ram it home with a ball-peen hammer."

Rubbing at his eyes, he willed the banging headache he was getting to go away. She was right. He was being a jerk. There'd be plenty of time for that later when they were haggling over custody and birthdays and…suddenly a thought occurred to him. "When was she born?"

Kara inhaled a short breath as if needing the strength, then answered, "September 17."

"That's my mother's birthday."

"I know."

If that didn't beat all… He shook his head. "I know you had your reasons and they probably seemed pretty solid at the time but…I wish to God you'd told me. That's all I'll say about it for the time being. But—" he eyed her solemnly and he almost detected a delicate shudder in her frame "—when this is all said and done…"

"I get it, Matthew." Whatever Kara was feeling was gone in the next minute when her gaze hardened and there was nothing but an FBI special agent left behind. "But for now, stow it. We've got work to do," she said.

Matthew smothered the grin that tugged at his mouth. For whatever it was worth, Kara Thistle had grown up to be one tough chick.

And, he kind of respected that.

Kara was onto something, she could feel it buzzing at the back of her skull, gnawing at her consciousness, demanding that she dig deeper.

And, there was something else, too. She couldn't deny it. She'd heard a child's voice singing even though she knew there was no one in the room aside from her. She'd never been the superstitious type, never one to believe in fairy tales or ghost stories, but it was hard to shake the idea that something otherworldly was in on this case. Was it Hannah's ghost? She shuddered at the thought and then immediately felt silly for even thinking it. Ghosts. She exhaled a short breath and shook her head at the ridiculous direction of her thoughts. But…the more she thought about it, the more there was no getting away from the fact that twice she'd heard things that couldn't be there.

She groaned and stuffed the rest of her Danish in her mouth. She'd brought it with her when she and Matthew had returned to her room to continue on with their work.

"What's wrong?" Matthew asked, looking up from the topographical map he was studying.

"Nothing," she grumbled. Like she was going to share *that* particular tidbit with Matthew. He'd think she was bonkers. Hell, she was one step away from thinking that herself. "Just frustrated."

He nodded, accepting her answer. "I know the feeling. How do you handle this kind of pressure day in and day out?"

"It's my job," she answered simply.

"Helluva way to earn a paycheck. How did you raise a child with the hours you keep?"

"I had Mai to help me." Kara leaned back in her chair but avoided making eye contact. Talking about Mai was hard now that she was gone. They'd become more than employee and employer; they were friends. "I met Mai in Chinatown. I was looking for an address on a perp we were tracking and she was looking for work. She just so happened to live in the building where we ended up and even though the perp wasn't there, I discovered she was looking for a nanny position. She was first-generation immigrant from Vietnam and she came here to make money for her family."

"Did she speak English?"

"Enough but her accent was pretty thick. For a while it was hard to decipher what she was saying but we worked it out and she came to love Briana like her own. I couldn't have asked for a better nanny than Mai." She pushed down the lump that had risen in her throat. It took a moment before she could continue. "I need to call her family. I'm sure they've already been contacted but I need to talk to them personally."

"She was a live-in nanny, I assume?"

Kara nodded. "Like you said, with the hours I keep, I needed someone who could be there 24/7."

"Doesn't leave much room for a life," he commented, and she bristled.

"Mai loved her job and I paid her well. I paid her enough to eventually move her family from Vietnam to here."

"I wasn't talking about Mai," he corrected her softly, and her ire deflated like a punctured tire.

"Sorry. I guess I'm a little defensive about that. It was something I worried about with Mai but she always assured me she loved her job and had more time off than she needed. But you're right…neither of us have…had… much of a life to speak of. Briana was at the center of both our worlds. If Mai had survived, she'd likely be suicidal right now. She'd blame herself over what happened."

"Like you?"

Unexpected tears sprang to her eyes. How did he still know her so well after all these years? She blinked away the moisture but gave a jerky nod.

"It's not your fault," he said gruffly, and she looked at him in surprise.

"How is it not? I led this maniac straight to her. I put her in harm's way with the very nature of my job."

"Don't go there. I'm sure you are a good mother."

"How can you say that when I've kept her from you all these years?"

He looked at her squarely. "I said you are a good mother…not a good person. And I can say that because I know you, Kara. You have a loving heart—if not always the best judgment."

"Gee, thanks."

He shrugged. "You asked."

"You're right, I did. I won't make that mistake again."

He chuckled in spite of the tense set of her shoulders, and the sound reached deep down into the pit of her belly and warmed the chunk of ice settled there. A grudging smile followed. So much had changed, yet Matthew at his core remained the same. Solid, dependable…and a straight shooter.

"Do you miss Neal?" she asked, knowing full well she should probably steer clear from that discussion, but what the hell, she figured. She was curious as to his answer.

"Of course I miss him. He was my best friend. Do you miss him?" There was an edge to his voice but Kara didn't take offense. She'd expected as much. "You're the one who left him behind, not me."

"I didn't leave Neal behind," Kara said softly. "He chose to stay."

"Whatever."

"What's that supposed to mean?"

"Kara, Neal told me what happened. There's no need to try to clean it up for my sake."

She stared at him. "What the hell are you talking about?"

The hard edge returned to his eyes and his mouth tightened. "Kara, you left Lantern Cove behind when you no longer had any use for it. You used Neal to get into the department and to put you through school to get your degree. Then when you got accepted into the bureau, you split. It doesn't take a rocket scientist to figure that one out, but Neal told me that when you left you told him that you'd never loved him and you were glad to finally leave us all behind."

Kara could only stare. Neal said that? Why would he spread such lies? When Kara didn't say anything, Matthew continued with a curt shake of his head. "You destroyed him just as sure as that car took his life. You had to know that your words would've devastated him. You were his world."

Yes, she did know that. She'd carried the burden of that knowledge for years and finally had to stow it away in a deep, dark place in order to function after he died.

But she never would have imagined that Neal would spread lies about her to Matthew, of all people.

"And you believed him?" was all she asked.

"Of course I believed him." Matthew looked taken aback. "Why wouldn't I?"

She shrugged. "Why indeed." What was the point of dragging all this out now? Neal was long gone. But it rankled that Matthew thought so little of her character that he'd automatically believed something so awful of her when Matthew had always known her better than anyone—even Neal.

Her brain said let it go but she just couldn't. For some reason she couldn't let Matthew believe that she was that kind of person. It was bad enough she'd kept his daughter from him. She wasn't going to allow him to think she could've hurt Neal like that.

"I never said that to Neal," she said quietly, watching for Matthew's reaction. "He lied to you."

"Neal never lied to me," Matthew said, refusing to believe her.

"He did. Neal was a phenomenal liar. He probably would've made a decent operative in the CIA or some other agency where honesty is subjective to the situation. Did you know that Neal and I tested together for the bureau?"

Just as she knew it would, the news shocked Matthew. "What?"

"Yeah. Except he wasn't accepted. He didn't pass the psych test. I begged him to come with me when I left. I put my pride aside and *begged* him. He refused. He demanded—not asked—that I stay. He wanted me to choose between him and my career. I knew I couldn't stay here in Lantern Cove forever. It would've killed me."

There was another reason she desperately needed to get away and it had everything to do with Matthew. That night together had done more than create a child; it had sparked a hunger she'd never known was there and it had scared the shit out of her. She couldn't have feelings for Matthew. She was in love with Neal. And so she'd been eager to run.

"I figured after he calmed down, I could talk him into coming with me. But he died before I got the chance."

Matthew sat silent, the struggle apparent on his face, but there was anguish there, too. She knew what he was feeling. She'd seen sides of Neal that were hidden to the world. Love was blind but somewhere, deep down, Kara had known that Neal's character was weak. But it was so easy to forgive him his little transgressions, for Neal had a way of charming the skin from a snake.

"Why didn't you tell me?"

She barked a short, mirthless laugh. "Tell you what? Would you have listened?" She shook her head and said, "Don't kid yourself. You were just as loyal to Neal as I was. You never would've listened and I didn't want to drive a wedge between you. I figured you and I had done enough damage."

It was the first time she'd mentioned their night together. Sure, it was there between them because they'd already acknowledged that they'd made a child as a result, but neither had mentioned the reason they'd fallen into each other's arms that long-ago night.

The memory should have been distant and faded with the passage of time but it had never lost its power to make her draw a sharp breath each time she ventured there in her mind.

That in itself had always bothered her. She'd always chalked it up to guilt, that her mind wouldn't let her forget because she was ashamed for betraying the love of her life with his best friend. But being here with Matthew again made her wonder if the reasons were different.

Fabulous timing, she thought darkly.

"Did you tell Neal about us?" Matthew asked.

She shook her head vehemently. "God, no. I wanted a life with him. I doubt that would've gone over very well. Why? Did you tell him?" she asked, suddenly very keen to know if Neal had gone to his grave knowing how they'd betrayed him.

To her relief, Matthew said, "No. I wanted to but I didn't. Still, sometimes I wondered if he somehow knew."

Kara brushed aside Matthew's speculation. "No. He'd have said something if he'd known."

"Perhaps."

Matthew's pensive look gave Kara an unsettled feeling in her gut. "What?"

"It's probably nothing." He paused as if he were waging an internal battle on what to say next—if anything at all—and then continued with a troubled grimace. "But the night he died...he did say something that has always bothered me."

Kara realized she was clenching her fists under the table and slowly loosened them. "What did he say?"

"He said, 'There are some things that we're just not meant to have.'"

A shudder rocked through her. So damn cryptic. And so like Neal. He'd always enjoyed playing with words. "I'm sure it doesn't mean anything."

"Probably not. He'd been drinking down at Tally's and was feeling pretty low. I tried to get him to go home and sleep it off but he assured me that he'd get a ride home soon. I was on duty that night or else I would've just stayed with him. That was the last time I saw him alive."

"He was drunk when he wrecked?"

"Yeah," Matthew admitted. "The only good thing is that he was probably so far gone he never felt a thing when the impact struck. At least, that's my hope."

She swallowed. "Do you...think it was suicide?"

Matthew's mouth tightened and he looked away. His answering shrug gave it away.

"You do."

He turned to look at her, his eyes full of pain and guilt. "Yeah. I should've seen it coming. He was so depressed, worse than I'd ever seen before. But somehow, I thought he'd pull through."

"It's not your fault," she murmured, but there was guilt for her, too. "Neal made his own choice." The words were easy to say but she knew it wasn't that simple to believe them. Still, she said them, anyway.

Silence sat between them for a long moment, then Kara ventured, morbid curiosity getting the best of her, "You said…his last words were of me…what did he say?"

Matthew looked so sad that Kara felt an undeniable pull to go to him but she resisted. She didn't know how well that kind of action would go over with Matthew and she wasn't up to being rejected in her current emotional state. Matthew sighed, then shook his head. "Listen, I shouldn't have said that earlier. I was just being vindictive. Forget I said it."

"I want to know what he said."

"Do you really?" Matthew asked, peering at her intently. "I mean, what purpose will it serve? You and I have spent years beating up on ourselves for what happened to Neal and under the current circumstances, I don't see the point of piling more emotional baggage on you."

"It's important to me to know," she said.

He seemed resigned and none too happy about it. That in itself gave Kara an odd lift to her spirits. He cared—deep down and probably buried under a wealth of animosity— but he still cared about her. An unexpected show of tears sprang to her eyes. *Shit.* Suddenly, she didn't really want to know what Neal had said. It would probably haunt her forever and she'd had enough of that crap to last a lifetime. "You're right. I don't need to know," she said softly. She wiped at the moisture surreptitiously but Matthew caught the action.

"Are you all right?" he asked.

"No. I'm not," she answered honestly. "My kid is missing and in the hands of a psycho baby killer and on top of all that, all these past history revelations are seriously hard to handle. I feel like I'm going a bit crazy." Stark, raving mad was more like it but she wasn't about to admit that.

An off-kilter smile formed on his lips. "I'd be worried if you somehow managed to take all this in stride. It's okay to admit that you're barely holding your head above water. It won't make you a lesser person in anyone's eyes."

Easy for you to say. A chuckle escaped but there was a mournful quality to it that she couldn't hide. "Well, I'll keep that in mind," she said with a small shrug that said the exact opposite.

Matthew reached out and tucked a loose strand of hair behind her ear. The action, slow and deliberate, ignited a heat deep in her belly that she fought hard to douse but it kindled brighter when she dared to meet his stare.

They held each other's stare for what seemed like forever. Thoughts that raced suddenly stilled and Kara didn't even question her desire—no, need—to go straight into his arms.

Thick bands of muscled forearms wrapped solidly around her, tucking her against a heart that beat hard and strong inside his chest. Kara rose on her tiptoes to press her petite length against his tall frame. She angled her head and he took the invitation without hesitating.

His lips, firm and commanding, anchored to her mouth in an assault that left her dizzy, aching, and needing the very thing that she'd denied herself for years.

Sex, a heated voice whispered in her fevered brain. It'd been so long. Firm hands cupped and kneaded the flesh of her ass and pressed her tightly against the hardened ridge teasing her most sensitive spot. She gasped against his mouth and clung tighter. A whimper escaped as his mouth grazed the tender skin of her neck and she cocked her head at a deeper angle to give him better access. He obliged and sucked the flesh into his mouth, sending a dark thrill cascading through her body until she writhed against him with a demand for more.

Falling to the bed, they divested each other of their clothes in short order. Kara didn't waste precious time allowing herself to consider the ramifications of what they were doing. She was too far gone to care. She needed him inside her, to feel him filling and stretching her, sliding and pounding until an orgasm burst from her body. She would have this and nothing would stop her from getting it.

"Kara," he rasped against her mouth, his hands stilling hers as if he were going to try to talk some sense into the both of them. She growled and sucked his tongue into her mouth.

"No talking," she whispered when she finally freed his mouth from her own assault. "Please."

The last part came out a tortured plea and he responded with a nod of understanding. For a brief moment she wondered if he sensed her desperation in her touch, felt the despair coming from her heart in waves, and instinctively knew she needed to touch and be touched if only for this moment in time so that she could gather the strength to face what was coming.

Whatever it was, he understood and it alternately buoyed and sank her. This man had always known her and there was no escaping that. Not now. Perhaps not ever.

Kara's soft skin slid like skeins of satin beneath his fingertips and like a starving man, he couldn't get enough of her. Her scent, the sweet, feminine sounds she made as he explored her body, the absolute perfect matching of their bodies—it was like hell in the most wonderful way.

He bit back a groan as he sank into her slick, hot folds, and his heart threatened to burst from his chest from the raw emotion. Her legs wrapped around his torso and she clung to him like she was a woman about to die and he was her savior.

Framing her face between his hands, he claimed her mouth, lips swollen and red, as he slowed his tempo to a torturous pump and grind. Seated to the hilt, he sucked in a wild breath as she clenched her inner muscles tightly, making the withdrawal motion that much more pleasurable.

He pulled back and gently placed her legs over his shoulders, the beauty of her spread before him nearly stealing the strength from his limbs. Penetrating deep, he rocked her body, hitting that sweet hidden spot with unerring accuracy, until she let loose with a keening wail that she couldn't hold back as every muscle in her body tensed and then melted.

Knowing she'd reached her release, Matthew quickly found his until they both collapsed to the bed, sweaty and sated.

The first thought that came to him as he slowly regained the ability to think was startlingly blunt.

What the hell have you just done?

Chapter 11

Kara retrieved her discarded clothing and quickly dressed, all the while suffocating under the silence in the room.

"This is awkward," she finally admitted, averting her eyes while Matthew finished buckling his belt. He spared her a short look that was in total agreement and she felt her cheeks heat. "Seems like old times." In so many ways.

"You got that right," he muttered, jerking his pant legs over his boots. Straightening, he raked a hand through his dark hair and his mouth tightened to a grim line. "Where do we go from here?" he asked.

She pulled her hair into a low, no-nonsense ponytail and reverted to her fail-safe: professionally distant. "We go back to where we were before." Perhaps he wouldn't notice that she was spewing total bullshit. Already she could feel that her words were disingenuous but she couldn't afford to let herself weaken. She needed to be focused and strong for Briana.

He gave her a caustic look that made her wince privately. "Is it that easy for you?" he asked.

"Is what easy?"

"Pretending that you don't have feelings?"

Her nerves, already stretched to the breaking point, snapped. She turned on him. "What do you want from me? You want me to fall into a sobbing heap just so you can see that I'm hurting inside? Or would you rather I just fall over you in the hopes that you'll take pity on me and allow me to cry on your shoulder?" She didn't wait for an answer. "Not gonna happen, Matthew," she said coldly.

"I wasn't talking about the way you handle yourself in a crisis," he shot back, advancing toward her, his face darkening and losing all traces of the lover she'd just been with. "I'm talking about us. *This*." He gestured between them in a jerky motion. "We just made love yet you're acting like we were two drivers in a fender-bender and now comes the tedious insurance exchange."

"We had *sex*. Don't read more into it than the situation deserves." She nearly flinched at the wintry chill coming from her voice but it wouldn't do either of them any good to think that there was more between them than a physical need created under extreme circumstances. "And it was good," she admitted, throwing him a bone. More than good. Damn near fantastic. "But there is no us."

His gaze narrowed but he remained silent. His silence unnerved her but she didn't let it show. She swallowed and eyed him intently. "Are we clear?"

"Oh, yeah. *Perfectly*."

She suppressed a shudder. She was going to hell. And by the look on Matthew's face, he'd be the first to throw the going-away party. Jerking his coat on, he stalked to the door. Hand on the knob, he gave her a cruel smile and said, "In that case…thanks for the screw."

* * *

Matthew cursed under his breath as he drove away from Kara's motel. What level of stupidity had he sunk to? One that was pretty far to the bottom. To sleep with Kara again? He slammed the Jeep into gear roughly, ignoring the vehicle's screech at the treatment.

The original Ice Bitch, that's what Kara was. She didn't have an ounce of human compassion in her lean body. And he already knew that, so what was his excuse for taking her to bed?

The short answer was easy even if it stung. He'd always wanted Kara. Even when she'd been off-limits. That's why he'd given in all those years ago when she'd come to him, crying, clinging to him as if she needed his strength to keep her going, just like tonight. And just like tonight, he'd hated himself for succumbing to his baser desires. Betrayed a friend. Took his girl into his arms and loved her with more than his body, trying to communicate all those years of longing and secret hope that maybe she might see him as more than a friend someday, only to routinely quash that dream when he saw Kara with Neal. The smile that wreathed her face when she was around him was proof enough that he should keep his trap shut and try to bury those feelings so deep it would take a deep-sea drilling team to unearth.

He slammed his hand against the steering wheel. Damn it! He wanted to hate her. He had plenty of reason. His daughter—the word felt strange and foreign on his tongue yet pain and fear arced through him just the same—was in danger and he couldn't let his feelings cloud his judgment. *Too late for that.* Blowing a sharp breath, he jerked the wheel, spewing gravel from the shoulder as he did an abrupt U-turn and headed back to Kara's motel. She wasn't going to keep him from helping in this investigation. He didn't care what she said. She wasn't in charge anymore. She was just like him—a parent living in fear of the worst possible outcome.

Kara had only just wiped at the moisture gathering at the corners of her eyes when Dillon walked in, his eyes stormy.

"What was that all about?" he asked.

She feigned ignorance to buy time. "What are you talking about? And I thought I asked you to knock."

"Beauchamp just drove out of here like the devil was on his heels. What happened?"

"Nothing."

"You're lying," Dillon said, deadpan.

She shrugged. "It has nothing to do with the case so drop it."

"You said he wasn't going to be a problem," he said, stubbornly refusing to do as she requested, which was so like Dillon. He never did as one asked unless it suited him. She heaved a sigh and turned away but Dillon wasn't ready to let it go. "Contrary to what you think at the moment, pissing off the locals in high places isn't the way we've been trained to work in these kinds of situations. You said you could put the past behind you but it seems you were wrong."

She turned to face Dillon, unable to stop the tears from flooding her eyes but she blinked them back to prevent them from falling. "I made a mistake, okay? I…" She needed someone to hold on to, someone to make this horrible pain go away, not just someone…Matthew. "It won't happen again," she finished, swallowing whatever might've been poised to fall from her mouth before it could destroy the careful wall she was trying to build.

"Why don't I believe you?"

She ground her eyes with her palm. "I'm exhausted, Dillon. I don't have the strength to play this game with you. You're not in interrogations any longer, remember?"

He ignored that last part, his gaze boring into her until Kara was tempted to punch him simply because she had a lot of pent-up emotion backing up in her system and he was giving her shit when she plainly told him to back off.

"I know Matthew is Briana's father," he said simply and she startled.

"Excuse me?"

He shrugged. "It's my job to know things. I've known since we got here and I met the chap. Honestly, Kara, it doesn't take my skill in observation to see that. Briana looks just like him. I'm not here to niggle your nuts about the fact that you kept his daughter from him. I'm sure you had your reasons at the time, but now that the cat is out of the bag, so to speak, there's no need to muddy the waters further by poking at him. This case is highly sensitive. Colfax is riding my ass so hard I've got his handprint on my cheeks but I'm willing to take the heat for you and Briana. Don't make it harder than it already is."

"I'm not trying to," she said.

"Well, you're doing a bang-up job from where I'm standing of doing the exact opposite. What happened between you two that sent him barreling out of here?"

"I appreciate what you're saying but I don't want to get into this right now."

"Did you sleep with him?"

"No."

He assessed her openly and she bristled, probably because she'd just lied through her teeth and it was a stupid move because Dillon could see the truth in her body language. "All right, yes, but it won't happen again," she snapped. "Don't you have some work to do?"

Dillon gave a minute shake of his head that was fairly contained even when she knew that he was disappointed. He headed for the door. "I hope this time you used birth control," was all he said before he closed the door behind him.

Her anger was misplaced and she knew it. She wasn't angry with Dillon. He was doing his job while she was mucking everything up. He was covering for her with Colfax and shielding her from the angry calls coming from Senator Nobles. She knew this. Yet...the rage she felt bubbling under the surface for her own screw-up took advantage of the situation to find a victim. She'd apologize later. Right now, she needed to move. Quickly changing into running pants, she slid on a light jacket and headed for the beach.

It wasn't a beautiful day, not by the usual standards. The sun was sulking behind a veil of gray clouds and the mist coming from the water gave everything a damp chill. It was melancholy and bitter and absolutely perfect for the foul state of mind she was stuck in.

Breaking into a jog as soon as she hit the shoreline, she pounded the sand, puffing hard as the shifting sands sucked at her shoes and made the effort ten times harder. The burn in her calf muscles was more welcome than the ache in her heart and she pushed herself harder. She knew why Tana ran until her lungs nearly disintegrated; it was to dull the pain that was always there. Just as Tana couldn't escape her past, neither could Kara.

This place—so a part of her—was something she tried to forget. Neal and Matthew were part of her past but Briana was her future and everything that was good and beautiful in her life. Yet, Matthew was a part of Briana, so the very thing she'd avoided for ten years had come to bite her in the ass. Her past was intruding on her future and yet…she couldn't say that a tiny part of her hadn't always wanted to share the joy of being Briana's parent with Matthew. It was just that the self-preservation part of her had always been stronger.

She was a coldhearted bitch. If only that were totally true. The thing is…if she truly were as coldhearted as Matthew surely believed, she wouldn't be running away from the pain that was tearing her in two over the look Matthew had given her as he walked out. She'd hurt him and she knew it. Just as she knew she'd hurt him that night when she made him promise not to tell Neal. She'd chosen Neal over Matthew and she'd be a liar if she didn't admit that there were many nights when she'd wondered if she'd made the wrong choice.

Neal. She collapsed on the ground, her hands curling in the cold, moist sand as she fell forward until her forehead rested against her clenched palms. How did three best friends end up destroying one another so completely?

She'd inadvertently created a love triangle that she'd never been aware was there until that night when she and Neal had had the worst row ever. It was the night Neal had demanded she stay when she knew in her heart she couldn't. A part of her had been so angry that he'd discounted her dreams so easily because of his damn ego but mostly she'd been crushed. Turning to Matthew hadn't been a conscious choice but she'd run to him unerringly. And something had clicked inside her that had never fully come to life with Neal, and God, it had scared her.

Just like she was scared right now.

What if she'd never truly loved Neal at all? Not in the true sense. The kind of love that was bone-deep and uncompromising; the kind that made a person feel whole

and complete for the gift of that love in return. Had Neal
loved her that way? No. But she suspected Matthew had.

Had. Past tense. *Shit*. Way to really screw things up.
Again.

Chapter 12

Kara wiped the sweat dotting her hairline as she returned to the room where the team was assembled. The motel was small, which had enabled Kara to basically commandeer the entire establishment for their purposes. She didn't need to worry about civilians poking around and it allowed them to set up the command base without fear of tampering or theft. But at that moment, "small" had its downside.

She nearly skidded to a stop as her gaze collided with Matthew's, as she hadn't expected him to be there after the ugly scene in her own room. Her cheeks flushed uncomfortably. She pulled her gaze away from him to focus on something else, but he seemed to dominate the room.

"Colfax scheduled a press conference," Dillon stated, his frown deepening. "Reporters caught a hold of the fact that Hannah Linney was found."

"Damn," she swore under her breath but what could she expect? It had only been a matter of time before the press caught wind of the recent body dump. "When and who?"

"We were just going over that when you came in. We figured Zane might be a good spokesperson for the team since you're no longer an official member for the time being."

She looked to Zane, who appeared visibly discomfited. "That okay with you?"

He shrugged. "I guess, but I don't understand why we have to talk to the press at all. It's an open investigation... the press could muck it up."

She sighed. "Yeah, well, Colfax is a media whore. We all know this. It's the kinder, gentler bureau these days and it's all about the new image, right? Don't waste energy fighting it. When's the conference?"

"Three o'clock at the police station," Dillon answered, and Kara checked her watch.

"That gives us an hour to prepare a statement and prep you for the questions you can't answer. Also, I want surveillance in the room just in case this psycho decides he wants a front-row seat. I'm sure his ego would appreciate the attention."

"Sort of like when killers attend their victim's funerals," Tana threw in with a disgusted curl of her lip, but then she snapped into work mode efficiently. "You want all exits monitored?"

"You know it." Kara said, and looked to Zane. "C'mon, Hollywood star. Let's get you ready for your big debut."

"Shut up," he growled, and she laughed. "Dillon's the one the women swoon over. He should be the one doing this."

"Yeah, well, Dillon put you in the hot seat so quit complaining and let's get to work. You've got a lot to learn in an hour."

Kara glanced Matthew's way almost involuntarily before leaving the room, but was relieved when she saw that he was talking with Tana about the security of the police station. His solid frame looked overpowering next to Tana, even though she wasn't exactly short. She was beginning to feel a need for his presence even though she had the urge to run the other way. Hurrying from the room, Kara slammed the door behind her.

Matthew felt rather than saw Kara leave the room. He was speaking with Tana when Kara left with the reluctant agent. His chest, tight from the breath he was holding on to, loosened as he relaxed. He hadn't meant to tense up but the moment she entered the room, hair damp and nose pink at the tip, it was like all the oxygen in the room had been sucked into a vacuum.

He purposefully avoided looking at her but the effort was difficult. She'd been running, he surmised from the state of her clothes, yet another little tidbit about the new Kara that he didn't know. When they were teens Kara had hated running on the beach. It was something Neal had talked her into when he was going through his fitness phase that hadn't ended before he died. Matthew wondered why she continued when Neal was no longer around to cajole her into hitting the beach.

Of course, Kara hadn't needed to lose weight then, just as she didn't need to lose any now. He'd felt the skin sliding over the bones of her rib cage as he'd explored her body. Considering that she had very little body fat on her lean figure, he wondered why she punished herself with exercise.

"I heard you and Kara grew up together," Tana said, watching him with that steady, intense stare that probably unnerved people if they were feeling the least bit guilty about anything in their lives. When Matthew answered with a short nod, the blonde sighed. "Must've been nice growing up here by the water and the redwoods."

"Parts of it were great," he agreed. "Other parts...not so much."

"Like what?"

"The isolation. The Lost Coast area isn't what you'd call heavily populated, as you've already seen. People get a little peculiar when they don't get much interaction with the outside."

For a moment she seemed wistful as she said, "I don't know. I like the quiet. You could sit on the beach for hours and no one would bother you. It's nice." But then she seemed to realize she'd shared too much of herself and returned to professional mode with barely a blink. "Do you have working surveillance cameras in your conference room?"

"Well, first, I wouldn't call it a conference room, per se, but rather an oversized break room. And no, the only camera we have is in the holding cell and even that is iffy. Sometimes you have to give it a whack to convince it to get to work. I suppose your man over there has some extra ones we could set up," he said, gesturing to D'Marcus.

She nodded. "D'Marcus always comes prepared. He assumes that wherever we go, they never have the right equipment. The man would be naked without his electronics."

D'Marcus, hearing his name, swiveled in their direction, saying, "That's right. If I hadn't brought my treasure chest of goodies we'd be stuck using dial-up." He shuddered at the thought. "Instead, we've got state-of-the-art satellite Internet speeds courtesy of the United States government. Gotta love Uncle Sam for the toys we get access to."

In this instance, Matthew silently agreed, but under

normal circumstances, he didn't have much need for that high-tech stuff. He'd rather spend his free time on the water rather than plugged into anything electronic. He wondered if his daughter was more like him and enjoyed the simpler pleasures in life or if she was a city girl through and through. He fervently hoped he'd get the chance to find out.

Zane took to the small podium, if you could call it that. Scratched and worn, it looked as if it had been pulled from a storage closet. Zane gazed at the impossible number of journalists, both of print and television variety, without a hint of nervousness on his smooth face.

Kara gave him credit. The first time she'd hit the podium she'd wanted to throw up.

She scanned the room, making eye contact with Tana, then D'Marcus, reluctantly alighting on Matthew last. His face was tight, his shoulders tense, and like her, he was watching the room.

"I'm Special Agent Harris with the Federal Bureau of Investigations," Zane started, his voice firm and sure, giving the message that he was in charge and not the other way around. "At 0645 hours the body of nine-year-old Hannah Linney was discovered in a heavily forested area known as Wolf's Tooth. Hannah went missing almost a week ago from San Francisco. We are doing everything we can at the bureau to see that Hannah's killer is brought to justice. I'll now take questions."

He jerked a nod to the first reporter, a woman with a severe haircut and an unsmiling face. She was a bulldog in a linen jacket and Kara recognized her instantly: Gertty Ecker.

"Is it true the Linney child is a victim of the Babysitter?" Her sharp German-accented voice grated on Kara's nerves and she clenched her teeth. Do not answer that question, she mentally instructed Zane.

"We're not prepared to answer that question at this time. Next question."

Nicely done. But Gertty wasn't finished. As Zane directed his attention to another reporter, Gertty interrupted.

"Isn't it true the victim's body had similar ligature marks as the previous victims—" she did a quick check of her notebook "—Jason Garvin and Drake Nobles?"

Kara swallowed hard. Just hearing the names of the other children made Kara want to lose her breakfast all over the dingy tiled floor. In her imagination she heard Briana's name inserted among the victims and her legs threatened to buckle. Forcing down the bile burning her throat, she narrowed her gaze at Zane and gave a small shake of her head. *Do not answer that question. Move on.*

Zane answered without losing his composure. "I cannot comment on the nature of the victim's wounds at this time. Next question."

Suddenly, Matthew was at her side, a silent but solid presence that made her want to bury her face in his shoulder even though she didn't move a muscle or indicate that she even noticed he'd taken his place beside her.

"Seems to be holding his own," he whispered into her ear. She withheld the shiver but managed to nod. "Are all your people trained in media relations?"

"No."

He digested that information, then said, "Guess you're a good teacher then."

"Zane is a fast learner."

Matthew fell silent and they both continued to scan the room. No one stood out in Kara's estimation, but it had been a long shot that the killer would show himself in such tight quarters. The exits weren't easily accessed and there weren't many options for him to slip in unnoticed.

But the desperate and scared parent in her had hoped that the asshole would slink in like the vermin he was. That way, Kara could take him down—hopefully with force. Her fingers actually tingled at the thought of pulling her Glock and plugging the sicko with a full clip.

God, this was why they didn't let the families of victims get too close to the investigation. Emotion screwed everything up. Made people get careless and stupid. Kara rolled her neck on her shoulders and cracked the bones with a satisfying but slightly painful pop and a few people standing in front of her turned and stared.

"Sorry," she muttered, and excused herself.

Matthew followed Kara into the hallway. She shuddered and her shoulders bowed under the weight of the situation. She seemed the complete opposite of the woman who had practically thrown him out of her room only hours earlier. The smart thing would be to turn around and leave her to deal with her pain privately, but it was Kara and he simply couldn't, even as much as he wished he could.

"You okay?"

She straightened and wiped at her eyes. "Fine. I just needed some air."

"The room is small," he acknowledged. "All those bodies makes it stuffy inside. We're not used to having that many visitors."

"Yeah, I noticed. The number of people in that room could equal the entire population during the off season," she quipped, though her voice was thin and flat, not at all like her usual tone. She looked away but not before Matthew caught the shine in her eyes.

"Kara…"

She waved him away, her voice choking. "Matthew, please…I need a minute."

"What you need is to stop pretending that no one around you means anything," he muttered even as he pulled her into his arms. He cursed himself for being seven times the amount of stupid but as she sagged against him, he caressed her hair and said in a harsh whisper, "We're going to find her."

Her knees buckled and he held her tighter. A low moan escaped, full of anguish and heartache only a mother could know, and Matthew felt it in his own heart as surely as if he'd been around Briana from the moment she was born. She looked up at him, her eyes red-rimmed and raw, and for the first time, he saw the person she'd once been before circumstances and time had hardened her into someone else. "What if she's in pain? He hurts them, Matthew. Oh, God…they're just babies and he hurts them and snuffs out their little lives as if they mean nothing because to him they don't…but to us…the parents…they're our reason for living. If we don't catch him in time…" She drew a choking breath and shook her head, unable to finish her sentence.

"Shh," he soothed, holding her fiercely. He wanted to break something. He wanted to put his fingers around the throat of the person responsible for these heinous crimes and squeeze so tightly their head popped off. But even if he didn't say it, they both knew time was running short. The Babysitter kept the victims for only a few days. The clock was ticking and they were no closer now than they were when they found Hannah Linney. Desperate to do something other than fret and panic, he set Kara away from him and forced her gaze when she seemed ready to collapse. "Listen," he said, "here's what we're going to do.

Tonight we're going to order in and we're going to go over every case file and piece of evidence and we'll keep going over it until something fresh jumps out at us. Got it?"

Something in Kara switched into a different gear and after a long moment, she slowly nodded. He knew she needed to keep her mind occupied, otherwise she'd go nuts. They were alike in that aspect, which was probably why they were both insomniacs.

Kara wiped at her nose and huffed a short breath. "Tally's still make those God-awful fish and chips?" she asked.

He nodded. "They're a staple around here."

"Great. Let's get enough for the team. If the work doesn't keep us awake the indigestion surely will."

He chuckled, fighting the urge to pull her back into his arms so he could press a quick, searing kiss on her lips, and the effort made the sound a little forced. She must have zeroed in on his brain waves, for the moment heated between them. Whether she realized it or not, the tip of her tongue darted out to slide across the soft, plump fullness of her lips and he sucked in a sharp breath. Her eyes widened ever so slightly. She took a slow step away from him, which was in direct opposition to the signals her body language was throwing, but he didn't hold it against her. He knew how she felt. It was an odd thing to want the very person you should steer clear from for very good and solid reasons.

"Matthew…"

"Don't."

"You don't understand," she started but he cut her off.

"No, you're wrong. I *do* understand. Too well. Trust me. Don't worry, we're on the same page. It's just…" *Old habits die hard.* "I don't know, difficult to walk away when I know what you're going through. No one should be alone during something like this. We're Briana's parents. She needs us to work together, not against each other."

"You're right." She nodded but the motion was stiff, communicating quite clearly how she was not ready to think of him as Briana's father just yet. He tried to be understanding but his nerves were frayed, too.

"I'll get the food," he offered, but his voice held an edge he couldn't disguise.

"You're mad at me," she said flatly.

He was going to let it go, just walk away and cool off, but he couldn't. "Yeah. I'm mad. She's my daughter, too. You need to get used to that fact right quick because I'm not going to walk away from her. Not now, not ever."

A shadow of guilt flickered across her lovely face and it almost silenced him but then it was gone in an instant. "I've had nine years to get used to that fact, Matthew," she said.

"No. You've spent the past nine years trying to erase me from your memory, but I imagine that wasn't so easy to do with Briana looking just like me. What did you tell her about me? About her father? Didn't she ever ask where I was?"

"I told her that you weren't ready to be a father," she admitted, looking away. "Eventually, she stopped asking."

He swore, hating the idea that his daughter thought he hadn't wanted her. Bitterness flooded his mouth. "That's cruel. You never gave me a chance."

"I know."

"Am I so awful that you couldn't stand the thought of anything having to do with me?"

"No," she whispered. If it weren't for the stark expression on her face, he would've called her a liar for her actions spoke louder. But as it was it looked as if he'd just filleted her heart and left it bloody and bare for the buzzards to pick at. "Matthew, I can't talk about this right now. Please let it go...for now."

It was a plea. And Matthew knew Kara didn't ask or beg. He choked down the angry retort that was coming and gave in to her request with a jerk of his head. He didn't trust the words that might come out of his mouth at the moment. Instead, he walked away.

Chapter 13

Kara stared at the paperwork in her hand. "Someone, if not Bernie then someone he knows, was tromping around Wilkin's Mine. The samples match," she said, handing the paper to Matthew.

The report came over the fax just as the team was choking down the last of Tally's fish and chips. Matthew pursed his mouth before tightening it to a fine line. "Damn it," he swore.

"You like him, don't you." Kara found it hard to fathom why anyone would like that old coot but it was apparent in the way Matthew was staring at the paper, his expression disappointed, that he held the man with a certain amount of regard.

"He's not a bad guy, Kara."

She stiffened. "He might be the one holding our daughter hostage."

"I'd be willing to bet my left lung, he's not," Matthew

countered. Kara heard D'Marcus cough conspicuously but it was Dillon who stepped in.

"There is that thing where we assume everyone is innocent until found otherwise and all that nonsense, but the evidence does beg for another go at the guy."

"He's a crazy old bugger but he's not a killer," Matthew said.

"And just how many killers have you had tea with lately?" Kara asked, pinning him with a short glare. When he merely narrowed his stare, she continued with a sigh. "I don't mean to hurt your feelings but this isn't your forte. I'd be willing to take your judgment at face value if we were tracking down a pot grower but in this situation you have little to no experience. Sorry." She turned to Zane. "We'll need backup. This guy isn't what you'd call social."

Matthew blew a short breath. "I'll go with you. I might be able to get him to come in without having to manhandle him."

Kara gave her assent but wondered why Matthew was so protective of the man. She wanted to ask but she wouldn't do it in front of everyone. She sensed Matthew preferred to keep that information private. Otherwise he would've just come out and stated why he felt a soft spot for him.

Shaking herself loose from the curious musings, she refocused quickly and asked Tana, "Any luck with the universities? Anything come up out of the ordinary?"

Tana's look of frustration didn't bode well. "Not really, but I don't know what the hell to look for. It's worse than trying to find a needle in a haystack."

"Keep trying. I don't know how to explain it but I have this feeling that there's something there," Kara said, rubbing at the pressure behind her eyeballs, which had begun to pound. Reaching into her bag, she pulled out a prescription bottle and cracked the top. Seconds later, she had tossed back a few of the pills and washed them down with lukewarm water.

"What's that for?" Matthew asked. It was a few seconds before it registered what he was asking until he gestured at the bottle she was stuffing back in her purse. "The pills."

"I get headaches."

"And you need prescription-strength pills to knock them out?" he asked, his brow furrowing in his disapproval.

"Matthew, I'm not asking for your permission to take a prescription. So drop it."

That must've been the clue for everyone to clear out, for Dillon made a show of checking his watch. "I say it's time we call it a night. We're spinning our wheels at this point. We'll come back tomorrow with fresh eyes. What say you?" He looked to Kara for agreement but he didn't exactly find it. She wasn't ready to stop. But one look at the weary and red-rimmed eyes of her team made her scale back the sharp retort that would've followed and she simply nodded. "All right then," Dillon said, gathering his notes as Tana, D'Marcus and Zane did the same. He looked to Kara. "Bright and early?"

"Is there any other way?" Kara asked with a fatigued smile, which he returned.

"Nope. Bright and early it is."

They all filed out of the room, Kara carrying an armful of case files to take back to her room, while Matthew carried another armful for her. They walked in silence until they reached her room.

She opened the door and flipped the light before depositing her files on the small table, directing Matthew to do the same. Her eyes were gritty from lack of sleep and sheer fatigue was beginning to make her thoughts slow. Matthew leaned casually against the door frame.

"Why the pills, Kara?"

"Why do you have a soft spot for Bernie Poff?"

A tiny smile tugged at his lips but he didn't answer. Stubborn man. Finally, she sighed. "I get tension headaches and regular-strength Tylenol doesn't do the trick any longer. So I take prescription-strength ibuprofen. You can stop looking at me like I'm some kind of closet drug addict." She crossed her arms across her chest and gestured. "Your turn."

Instead of answering, he moved toward her and slowly closed the door. Her heart rate kicked up a beat but she kept her face neutral, even mildly amused, at his actions. "What are you doing?" she asked.

"There are better ways to take care of a headache," he said, his tone deceptively mild, yet it sent a riot of goose bumps cascading down her back. In her mind she retorted with all sorts of witty comebacks but her mouth never actually moved. In fact, she'd become rather mute at the moment as the moisture left her mouth and fled south, slicking her with heat in seconds. She gave a mild shake of her head. Matthew smiled, slow and wicked, and then just as she was sure he was going to bend down and kiss her, he spun her around and slipped a chair under her butt.

"What are you doing?" she asked again, this time stunned and a little disappointed.

"Helping with your headache," he answered as his hands, big and sure, heavy and firm, started kneading the flesh between her shoulders. "The best way to get rid of a tension headache is to get rid of the tension, right?"

She gasped as he hit a tender spot. The pain mingled with the intense pleasure and she could barely get the words out as she answered between moans. "Yeah, I guess so. Oh, yeah, right there. Ummm." Her head lolled forward and he went to the column of her neck, gently massaging the tight, tense muscles cording her spinal column. Then he moved to the base of her skull and as he palmed her head with firm pressure, she nearly melted into a boneless heap. "When did you learn how to do this?" she asked when she could speak again.

He continued to lightly massage her shoulders again and if she'd been able she might have started to purr. She sensed him shrug as he answered. "One of Mari's talents other than singing was massage. She called it her backup plan. She taught me a few tricks of the trade."

"Way to go, Mari," Kara said dreamily, not caring in the least that another woman had instructed Matthew's hands. She just didn't want him to stop. "She sounds like a peach of a woman," she added.

"She had her good points," he agreed mildly, moving to her lower back, causing her to lean forward to give him better access. She heard him suck in a sharp breath as her jeans gaped a little and her cheeks actually colored. She'd forgotten about the low-rise waistband and the fact that she'd gone commando this morning. Not because she particularly liked going without underwear—frankly, she found that it made everything chafe—but she'd been in a hurry that morning and hadn't wanted to waste time rummaging through her bags to find her chones. She straightened slowly and looked back at him with embarrassment as she stood. "Sorry. I didn't mean to flash you or anything," she said.

His blue eyes channeled a coastal storm, deepening as stark need sparkled from the depths to drown her. "I don't recall complaining," he said, his voice soft and dangerous as he slowly stalked toward her.

"What are we doing, Matthew?" she asked, licking her lips, moving with him to the bed. Even as she shook her head, she was anticipating his lips on hers. "This isn't a good idea," she tried reminding him, yet desperately hoped he'd ignore her attempt at reason.

"I'm obligated to continue," he said huskily, nuzzling her neck until her knees buckled from beneath her and she tumbled to the bed.

"Excuse me?" she asked, shaking the cobwebs from her brain. "What do you mean? Obligated?"

He cocked his head at her with a short grin that was alternately adorable and damn sexy, and answered, "It's the second part of a surefire headache killer. The best part."

He stripped her of her shirt and soon after her bra, then sucked her nipple straight into his hot, hungry mouth. "I like this remedy," she gasped, arching against him to give him everything, offering her body as if he was a god and she was his sacrifice. She shuddered as he lavished attention on the other side, squeezing the flesh firmly, teasing the pebbled tip until she was drenched with desire and mindless with pleasure. "So much better than...than... pills."

"I told you," he murmured, nipping lightly at the puckered tips. "You should learn to trust me."

She groaned and threaded her fingers through his thick hair. "I'll keep that in mind."

He stripped and soon she had him in her hand, gripped tight and firm, the warm skin sliding like silk against her palm, and she wanted to taste him, to know him in every way. She took him into her mouth and his deep-throated, guttural moan sent tendrils of wanton need spiraling through her as she sucked, licked and tenderly caressed the thick, heavy sac. She worked him until a fine sheen of sweat coated his skin and his hands curled in the bedsheets. She knew he was close and a part of her wanted to push him over that edge but he didn't let her. With a growl, he pulled her to him and planted a searing kiss on her mouth before pushing her down to the bed and spreading her to his hot gaze. She twisted, not liking how vulnerable she felt, but his grip clamped on her thighs and wouldn't let her move. The loss of control made her buck to get loose but he roughly pulled her to him and buried his face into her hot, slick folds. He emulated the sexual dominance she'd exerted only moments before until the tables were turned and she was panting with every tongue thrust and wicked little tease against her clitoris. He took her to the brink then refused her, alternating the pressure and the tempo until she was practically begging—*begging, damn it!*—for that sweet, soul-shattering release.

Just when she thought she'd die from the exquisite torture, he flipped her over and covered her body with his own, cupping her shoulders with his forearms and sliding into her body with one hard, shudder-inducing thrust that sizzled every nerve ending and made her gasp with undisguised wanton pleasure. He whispered into her ear as he pumped into her, burying himself deeper so he hit that elusive, blood-engorged spot, causing stars to burst in her head as waves of pleasure rocked her body for an orgasm that seemed to go on forever. Dimly, from far off, she heard Matthew yell his release as he collapsed against her and they remained that way for a long moment until their heartbeats calmed and the sweat dried.

Finally, he moved and they faced each other on their sides. She was afraid to say anything for fear of ruining the fragile moment between them, so she remained silent. Perhaps he felt the same for he merely watched her from behind hooded eyes. A man shouldn't have such beautiful eyes, she thought. They were the eyes of a poet, someone who saw the world in brilliant hues and subtle shades. Funny, how she'd never really seen him in that way before. Neal had always been the dreamer, not Matthew. It made her wonder in what other ways she might have been blind. If only she had the guts to find out. That scared, silly part of her was in control again, and she made sure she kept her mouth shut until the coast was clear. Instead of asking something useful, she opted for conversational.

"You never answered my question," she said softly.

"Which question?"

"The one about Bernie."

"Ahh." He sighed and rolled onto his back and she followed, settling comfortably into the crook of his arm. "Well, I guess you could say he saved my life."

She raised her head to stare at him. "How's that?"

"It was right after Mari and I split up. I was doing a lot of hiking back then to clear my head and I slipped and fell down a steep ravine, one a lot like Wolf's Tooth, and it just happened to be on the fringe of Bernie's property. Broke my ankle pretty bad. Bernie hauled me up out of that ravine and drove me to town so they could airlift me to Garberville. If he hadn't come along…I'd probably have died down there."

She shuddered at the thought but said, "That doesn't mean he couldn't be a killer just because he succumbed to a moment of kindness."

"He could've split as soon as he left me at the helicopter pad but he drove all the way to Garberville to make sure I was all right. He didn't have to do that."

"Maybe he was worried you were going to sue because you were injured on his property," Kara suggested. Matthew immediately disagreed.

"I don't buy that. He cares about people, he just doesn't want anyone to know it."

Kara digested the new information and shrugged. "Okay, maybe your instincts are correct but we still have to question him. The evidence demands it."

"I know," he acknowledged grimly. "Just do me a favor…don't judge the man before you hear the facts."

She started to protest but she was suddenly too tired to put up a front. She was so eager to find Briana and whoever was behind this nightmare she was ready to crucify the first suspect in her line of sight. "I'll let the evidence point the way," she said, knowing that was the best she could give at the moment. But she added with brutal honesty, "Just remember, if he's guilty…I'm going to nail him to the wall."

Matthew's voice hardened. "Kara, if he's guilty, I'm going to do worse than that."

Chapter 14

Early next morning, Matthew zipped his wool coat and walked up to Bernal Poff's front door. Kara followed a heartbeat behind, her gaze roaming the area for anything that might seem out of the ordinary.

Aside from the usual sounds of a redwood forest, it was devoid of human presence.

"Maybe he's at the mine," Kara suggested, glancing around. "Is it close by?"

"Not really. It's a pretty good hike from here."

"Well, let's hit it then. I'm wearing my hiking boots."

Matthew nodded. "Let's head out. I don't want to get caught outside when the next storm hits," he said, glancing at the sky. "I say we have about two hours before the skies crack open and we're soaked."

Kara agreed. "I think you're about right. Lead way."

They trudged east, deep into the mountain, winding their

way down a narrow, barely there trail and concentrated on keeping their footing. Soon, Kara was breathing hard, in spite of being in pretty good shape. But, she realized, running on the treadmill was nothing in comparison to scaling uneven terrain, wearing heavy boots, a pack and a wool jacket.

Matthew glanced back at her, his skin ruddy from the brisk air and asked if she was all right.

"My lungs and thigh muscles are screaming but I'm not about to collapse. Don't worry, I can keep up."

He gave her a smile and she actually felt herself returning it, but that smile quickly faded as they came into view of the gaping maw stuck in the hillside that she surmised was Wilkin's Mine. "Looks like something out of a Stephen King novel," she said, shuddering. "Creepy. You couldn't pay me to spend time down there recreationally."

"Yeah, it's not pretty but Bernie feels at home here. Stay put a minute. I don't want you to lose a foot or something in one of his booby traps."

Ugh. She was pretty attached to the idea of her limbs and appendages staying right where they were. "Good thinking."

"Bernie…it's Matthew Beauchamp." Matthew cupped his hands and hollered down into the cavernous opening. "If you're down there, I need to talk with you. It's important."

Silence met his request and Kara shifted with impatience. A fine layer of mist had started to settle from the top of the mountain like a thick foggy shawl that draped the trees until they disappeared beneath it. That mournful feeling returned, the same one she'd felt when they'd returned to Wolf's Tooth to look for missing evidence. Shoving her gloved hands into her jacket, she tucked her chin into the collar and pushed the irrational thoughts out of her mind—they were giving her the heebie-jeebies. Lack of sleep was catching up to her. She turned away from Matthew to look the way they'd come and nearly swallowed her own tongue at what she saw—or thought she saw—for within a heartbeat it was gone.

A child. Tattered and bruised. Dead. Staring at her. Beseeching her with mournful eyes to help her, though help was clearly beyond Kara's capabilities.

Shaking so hard she could've sworn her knees were knocking, she didn't realize Matthew was behind her until he was at her side.

She jumped. "Don't do that!"

"Don't do what?" He frowned. "What's wrong? You're as white as a ghost."

"Why'd you say ghost?" she queried sharply, knowing she was sounding like a lunatic, but that was okay because, frankly, she might truly be one. First she was sensing things that weren't there in her motel room, then hearing voices that weren't there and now…seeing dead kids that clearly weren't there. Shit. She was losing her mind. Great timing. "We should go," she said, unable to hide the quiver in her voice.

Matthew gripped her shoulders and peered into her eyes, searching for an answer that she wouldn't give him. Couldn't, actually because hell, she didn't know what was going on, either. "What scared you? Did you see something? Or someone? Kara…what's going on?"

Her eyes watered before she could stop them. She wanted to tell him so that he could give her a rational explanation and she could stop worrying about some kind of early-onset dementia crowding in but she couldn't get her mouth to say it. "I…I'm not comfortable here. What if there are wild animals? I think we should leave and come back later. With backup."

Matthew seemed dissatisfied with her answer but didn't press. "It looks like he's not here so I guess it wouldn't hurt to leave and come back. I don't really want to wait out the storm on this mountain, either. Let's head out. Watch your step," he instructed sternly, taking the lead.

It was hard not to cling to him as they passed the spot where the girl had been standing. Resisting the urge to squeeze her eyes shut just in case whatever she saw decided to make a second appearance, she forced herself to stay wide-eyed and alert.

In spite of her best efforts, her gaze was drawn to the spot. Something caught her eye. Only this time, it wasn't otherwordly. It was very real. "Matthew, wait," she called out, causing Matthew to turn.

"What's the matter?"

She pulled a plastic evidence bag from her small pack and slid on a pair of gloves. A twisted strand of rope—hemp by the looks of it—lay almost hidden in the bracken, nearly lost on the forest floor. Her heart thundered in her chest. "Does this look out of place here?" she asked, her voice shaking.

He looked grim but hopeful. "Yeah…it does. How soon can we get DNA results from the lab?"

"How fast can you drive?"

Matthew drove like the devil was on their heels. He spared a glance at Kara who still hadn't lost the sickly pallor leaching the color from her cheeks. Something had spooked her out there. Something she didn't want to admit.

"How'd you know that rope was there? It was barely visible. We obviously walked right past it the first time."

"Luck," she answered with a swallow and a shrug

that couldn't have been more fake. "Sometimes you get a break."

"Bullshit, Kara." He'd called her bluff and she shot him a dark look. "Just spit it out. What's got you so freaked out?"

"Matthew, what difference does it make how I saw it? What matters is that I found it, right?"

"I suppose."

She heaved a short, restrained breath and returned to staring out the window.

Dissatisfied and on edge, Matthew returned his attention to the road. The woman was impossible. But she had a point. If not luck, then what would have caused her to go to that very spot and find that damn piece of rope? His mind was blank. Kara was probably right. The how of it didn't really matter as long as it got them closer to finding Briana—in time.

Briana's captor had exchanged the gag in her mouth for a blindfold across her eyes so all she could see were shafts of light at the edge of the cloth and her own feet. Cold, runny oatmeal was shoveled into her mouth so hard that the spoon cut into her tender gums but she didn't cry out in pain. Briana quickly learned that her captor enjoyed when she cried, so she made a point to hold back her tears and silence her cries. She strained her ears to listen for anything that might give away where she was at but so far she'd heard nothing. No cars. No people. Just the occasional airplane overhead. And birds. They reminded her of Gracie Isaac's pigeons that she kept on her roof. Gracie had invited a few of their classmates over for a birthday party and had shown everyone her birds. They pooped a lot but the sound they made was sort of nice.

Briana swallowed hard and lifted her chin against the fear trapped in her chest. Birdsong was the only nice thing at the moment.

Kara thrust the evidence bag containing the scrap of rope into Tana's hands with tense instructions to get it to the lab. "Put an ASAP on that," Kara said, her nerves ready to snap. "I want the results back by this evening."

"I'll do my best," Tana said solemnly, and hurried from the room to hit the FedEx truck before it left town.

"How'd you find it?" Dillon asked.

"Pure dumb luck," she answered, refusing to be completely honest because frankly, she didn't have time to deal with her partner thinking she was bonkers, too. "I just happened to look down at the right moment and saw something that looked out of place." She drew a deep breath. "It looks like the same kind of rope the Babysitter used in the other cases. Hemp, I think."

"Well, we are smack dab in hippie hemp movement headquarters," Dillon said with a hint of his usual mocking sarcasm. He turned to Zane. "Hit up the local hardware stores, even into Fort Bragg, and see who sells this particular brand of hemp rope. Then, we'll start culling receipts, see if anything stands out. Frequent purchases by certain individuals and whatnot."

Kara nodded. Sounded like a solid plan. Now, if only her hands would stop shaking. The strain must have been evident for she caught an assessing glance from Matthew. She moved away and busied herself with case files, but after a moment, she realized she needed space. Clutching the files to her chest, she made to leave but Matthew followed, taking the files from her hands. She began to protest but he silenced her with a look.

"You need to eat. Let's head over to Tally's for a spell." She grimaced at his suggestion.

"All you do is shove food down my throat," she muttered, adding, "And if I force down another order from Tally's, I might die from food poisoning. You forget, it's been a while, my stomach has lost its tolerance."

"Fine. You name the place," he said.

She didn't want to eat. She wanted to find answers but her head was beginning to throb and she'd be an idiot to refuse sustenance. Basic needs must be met. Still, she glared as she answered, "Fine. We can hit the store and get some sandwich stuff. I don't want to waste time sitting down in a restaurant. I want to go over the data D'Marcus has put together."

"Fine by me. But you know you can't keep this kind of punishing schedule. You're only hurting yourself physically and making it hard for your brain to function."

She cast a wry look his way. "I see you never outgrew that annoying habit of being incessantly logical. In case you haven't noticed, I'm running on pure emotion. That's high-octane shit and food's not high on my list."

"I can tell. Let's go."

Kara resisted the urge to bristle and say something completely uncouth and unwarranted for she recognized that he was right, even if it bothered her to admit it. Rolling her neck, she gestured to the cars parked in front and walked purposefully. "I'll drive."

He shrugged and followed.

"We shouldn't spend so much time together," Kara said as she climbed into the car. "My team is very observant. They're going to catch on that we have a history and I really don't feel up to answering questions." Kara snuck a look at Matthew, mildly bothered that she couldn't read him by his expression. "I mean—"

"I get it," Matthew cut in, his jaw tensing. "Drop it, Kara. No one is trying to resurrect the past. Just relax. If you drop from exhaustion you're no good to the team, which means you're no good to Briana. My daughter is my number one concern. Getting her home safely is my primary objective."

That stung for reasons Kara wasn't ready to examine. "Right. Good," she said briskly, yet her fingers tightened around the steering wheel as an unexpected ache bloomed behind her chest wall. *Oh, stop it. You should be relieved that you're both on the same page.* The logical part of her brain was having a pissing contest with…*crap*…her heart. And she wasn't sure who was winning but she sure knew who had a hold of her flapping mouth. She slid into one of the three parking spots and didn't wait for Matthew to follow. The cab of the car suddenly seemed too small, too confining, and she needed air. Drawing deep breaths that froze her lungs and made her shudder, she welcomed the physical sensation. It was better than the phantom pain that seemed to pierce her heart whenever Matthew was the one who put distance between them. It was okay when she was the one pulling away because Kara had control. It was completely different to be on the other side of that action.

"You coming?" Matthew asked, his brow furrowing in annoyance when she hesitated. She jerked a nod and he went inside. The cold in Matthew's eyes was nearly as frosty as the air she was breathing. She'd hurt him. That was Matthew's way of insulating himself from further pain. She'd seen that look years ago. She'd never forget it. Would she ever stop hurting the people in her life?

Chapter 15

By the time Matthew got home, it was nearing midnight. Tired as he was, sleep eluded him. Fear ate at him with sharp, feral canines, confusion rode him hard, and a bone-deep ache to have the one thing that was never his was his constant companion.

The years with Mari had almost convinced him that he was finally over Kara Thistle. But seeing her again after all these years showed him exactly how hollow that belief was. He should hate her. He had every reason. But he couldn't. And damn it, he couldn't help but want her in his life again. He longed to feel her skin sliding against his fingers, hear her soft moans in his ear and cradle her in his arms. But his longing was nothing short of a wicked dream that he was afraid was going to disappear once he realized none of it was real.

But the pain was real. That was the thing that served to

remind him that Kara was here, the situation was deadly, and the odds were against them.

Sinking onto his bed, he let his head fall into his hands. He understood the panic that pushed Kara to run herself ragged even though he didn't know his daughter and hadn't been able to be there for her up until this point. Fear squeezed his heart at the thought of her dying out there alone, in the cruel hands of a madman.

Never in his life had he felt so helpless, so impotent.

His shoulders shook silently as tears leaked from his eyes and hoarse cries made his nose run. He cried in a way that he'd never done before. It was ugly, raw and debilitating. The fear of losing his only child before getting the chance to know her, to teach and guide her, killed a part of him that he didn't even know was alive.

He dreaded coming upon his daughter's body the way he had with young Hannah Linney. Somewhere in San Francisco a father grieved for his little girl. Heaven help him, he didn't want to suffer a similar loss.

He wanted to see Briana smile. He wanted to walk her down the aisle. He'd missed so much, would fate take so much more from him?

He trusted Kara's talents; he knew she was the best. But not even the best have impeccable records. And time was running out. He thought of Kara, drawn tight as a bow, brittle as antique china, and wondered how she was keeping it together. But there were cracks in her veneer. He could see the tiny fractures in small gestures she was too tired to hide; he could sense the panic bubbling under the surface that she tried to cover up with her waspish tongue. He wasn't a man prone to spouting off poetry, he'd never been overly sensitive, but he'd always had an insight when it came to Kara, which was something Neal had never grasped. Neal had been the center of his own universe; he'd been too self-absorbed to notice he wasn't the only person who could shine. It felt traitorous to admit that, even if he was only admitting it in his head. God, why hadn't he questioned Neal when he'd told him that crock of shit about Kara leaving them all behind for selfish reasons? *Easy.* He'd been too devastated that she'd run away from what they'd shared. If *he* could have run, he might have, but he was too entrenched here, in this town, where this place was all he'd ever known, to take that first step. Plus, someone had to keep Neal together as he fell apart in spectacular fashion. It had been like watching a star fall from the sky in a blaze of sparkling lights and knowing that as soon as it hit the earth the ground would snuff it out. *Awful.*

Grinding the residual tears from his eyes, he wiped his nose and kicked his shoes free from his feet before climbing into bed, still clothed and not caring, just needing to shut his eyes to escape the misery that hounded him. His last thought before sleep dragged him to nothingness was filled with desperate hope that they would close this chapter with joy instead of grief.

Kara tossed, kicking her blankets free from the tangle of her legs. Unable to find a comfortable spot, she stumbled from the bed to the sink but the glass was missing so she cupped her hands under the faucet and drank greedily. This was the worst part of being an insomniac. She often slept in fits and starts, especially so when she was working a high-profile case. She supposed she shouldn't have been surprised that sleep would elude her tonight.

Knowing that lying there would simply be a waste of time, she flicked on the light at her table and pulling her hair back, opened the case files. There was something she was missing. Something was staring her in the face.

After an hour, her eyes were watering from strain and she was ready to try the bed again. Sighing, she gathered the files and started putting them back in order when, out of desperation to leave no stone unturned, she reread the profiler's report that was done when the Nobles boy had been discovered. The senator had insisted on bringing in a consultant and the director had indulged him.

Frankly, Kara hadn't read it more than twice before moving on to other evidence. But as she scanned the paper, her heart rate quickened and she wondered if they'd overlooked something critical.

"Killer may have above-average intelligence and a superiority complex…"

She skimmed past the stuff that they had already figured out on their own.

Then she drew the paper closer and read one, seemingly small detail.

"The ligature marks suggest intricate knotwork, may suggest the need for small hands and nimble fingers."

That voice that whispered in her ear, possibly her sub-conscious, had been telling her all along.

They were looking for a woman.

Matthew showed up at Kara's room with doughnuts and hot coffee in an attempt to show that he was willing to let bygones be bygones but when she didn't open her door immediately as was her custom, he tried the door and found it open.

Kara, wild-eyed, fully dressed and looking like she hadn't slept in days, thrust a folder at him with a triumphant gleam. "Matthew…the Babysitter is a woman!"

Kara nearly went blind with the revelation, it was so monumental. All this time she'd thought they were dealing with a man because statistically serial killers were white, middle-aged men, but there were equally vicious and unstable women out there, too. What made it far more heinous was the very fact that most people didn't like to think of a woman intentionally hurting a child—maternal instinct or some such shit—but women hurt children all the time. Sometimes even their own.

She whipped around to stare at Matthew, who was watching her intently. "This is the missing key we've been searching for," she said. "I didn't see it before because, I'm ashamed to admit, I'd discounted the consultant that Nobles brought in. But the clue was there all along."

"Which is?" he asked, nonplussed but wanting to understand.

"Small, nimble fingers," she answered. "The knots in the rope, they left distinct marks on the skin. An expert said it could be a weaver's knot! I didn't think anything of it at the time because it was before we pieced together the connection to the nursery rhyme and it just seemed random. But now it seems to come together quite obviously. The weavers in the nineteenth century were typically women and children! How perfectly morbid for the killer to use a weaver's knot to tie into her sick little game. It's just one more little clue that she thinks we're too stupid to catch on to!"

"If you're right...this could be the break we've been hoping for," he said, his voice strained. "God, Kara, I hope you're right!"

Her eyes watered but only for a moment. Relief was sharp and immediate, and just the thing she needed to regain focus. Her vision cleared and for the first time in weeks, she was propelled by a feverish sense of purpose. This psycho bitch was screwing with the wrong person.

"Let's go," she instructed, not waiting to see if he followed. She knew he would.

"I have a very strong hunch we're looking for a woman," Kara announced to the assembled team as they rubbed at their eyes and downed coffee to jump-start their brains after a long night. "Go back to the university lists we've gathered of geniuses with a troubled past and narrow it down to the women. We're looking for someone with a history of either extreme activism, experimental procedures, disciplinary actions…someone with a criminal record. Anyone fits that description—pull it. Come on, people, time's wasting," she said.

Tana's expression was puzzled and Kara understood her concern; if she were on the other end…yeah, let's just say she got it. She looked to her friend and co-worker. "Trust me on this. I've got a feeling we're onto something," Kara said.

Tana nodded slowly. "I'd bet my life on the quality of your hunches. You've been right before. I'm on it," she said, moving into action.

Kara's eyes filled with moisture. Her team was more than her peers. They were her family. She turned to Matthew, who was conferring with Zane. Once finished, he returned to her side.

"I'm going to head back out to Bernie's," he said. "Something's not right. I've got a feeling, too."

"You think something's happened?" she asked.

He looked troubled. "Well, let's just say I'd feel a whole helluva lot better if I could just see that the old coot is all right. He rarely leaves the property except to get supplies, and when he does leave it's at the beginning of the month, not in the middle."

She could see his point. "Do you want me to come with you?"

He shook his head. "You stay here, follow up on that hunch of yours. I'll take Dinky or Oren out there for backup."

Kara's dubious expression must have said volumes for Matthew quirked an amused grin. "I'll be fine. Dinky and Oren are both crack shots even if they're not much on personality. You can reach me on the radio if you have any news."

As Kara watched Matthew leave, something warm and beautiful stole her ability to think for a rare second and she knew it came from him. She'd come to depend—once again—on his solid sense of logic and intellect. But like her, he wasn't one to waste time on things that couldn't be helped. Kara smiled privately at how alike they were, how alike they'd always been. But the moment was fleeting.

"I think I have something." The urgency in D'Marcus's voice erased all other thought as she moved to lean over his shoulder. "I've found a woman who fits your description in the database. I can't believe we missed it."

Chapter 16

Matthew and Oren followed the trail to Bernie's shack, both of them glad that the sun hadn't disappeared yet as it was wont to do during this time of year.

"I'm real sorry that you're tangled up in this mess," Oren said quietly, as they walked the path. The genuine sorrow in Oren's rough voice made Matthew jerk a nod in acceptance of the sentiment. "I never in a million years would've imagined that a case like this could have hit home so squarely."

Matthew nodded again, his throat tight. "Yeah. It's a helluva situation to be in." They walked in silence for a few minutes, then Matthew admitted his private fear to a man he considered a friend and a mentor. "I don't want to find my daughter like we found that other child. But I know time is running out. It almost seems...hopeless," he said, looking straight ahead as they continued to climb the mountainside. He didn't need to see Oren to know the man understood his pain.

"Don't think like that," Oren said gruffly. "Keep it in your head that you're going to find her alive and you hold on to it with your last breath. You hear me? Stop with the giving up. She's not dead yet. Don't start digging her grave before you have to."

Matthew nodded and they fell into silence again. Matthew felt mildly chastised but he deserved it. Oren had been a friend of his father's and had helped him get into the position he carried now. He respected the man and his counsel. When his father passed, Matthew found himself turning to Oren more often for advice, guidance. He wasn't ashamed to admit he didn't always have the answers. Oren was the kind of man who didn't begrudge him the questions.

"Been a long time since Kara Thistle was around these parts...how's that working out for you?" Oren asked.

"It's made things confusing," he admitted. *Confusing.* That was a mild word for the turmoil going through his mind. How about chaotic? Wretched? Nightmarish? Those descriptions were more fitting for the situation but Matthew kept his eyes on the trail and let it go at that.

"You know, Neal wasn't the only one who was a mess when she left," Oren said.

"What are you talking about?" Matthew bluffed, though why he even tried was a mystery. Maybe it was because Matthew didn't like to think of those days. He preferred to lock them away with a cache of other dark memories. The day Kara left, he could have sworn she'd physically hacked off a piece of himself and stuffed it in her luggage. Frankly, he'd been stunned by how hard it had hit him. He didn't want to talk about it then and certainly not now when there was plenty to worry about as it was. "If you're saying I was broken up about her leaving, you're wrong. Obviously, your memory is failing you. I hated her for leaving Neal the way she did. She's the one who twisted his mind. Maybe…" His voice trailed. He didn't have the stones to keep on that track when he knew it was all bullshit at this point.

Matthew lapsed into stony silence, which didn't seem to faze Oren at all. He continued, saying matter-of-factly, "I never did understand that woman's fascination with Neal. I know he was your best friend and all, but the kid was like an egg with a hairline crack. Eventually, that egg was going to bust open or go bad. That's just the way of things."

"Neal wasn't a bad guy," Matthew protested, mildly confused at Oren's statement and the direction of the conversation.

"Maybe. Maybe not. Who's to say at this point? The boy died before we ever got the chance to know. I'd say that's a blessing. Wouldn't you?"

Matthew shrugged, Oren's words hitting an uncomfortable chord. Matthew and Neal had been friends from the moment they met—something inside the two boys had connected and held fast. Matthew didn't think he'd ever be able to see past their bond to what was perhaps a bad seed deep down. The knowledge bothered him more than a little.

Finally, he answered Oren's question. "I don't know. But I'd be a liar if I said I didn't miss him. Having Kara around reminds me of everything in the past, both good and bad. Not quite sure what to think about that."

"Kara's the one who made something of herself when the chips were down. I can't imagine being pregnant and alone in a strange town with a new job is a situation many women could handle. Neal gave up—cracked under the pressure—with less to deal with other than his wounded pride."

"Did you know that Neal applied to the FBI?" Matthew asked, so startled at the possibility that he stopped and turned to look at Oren. He was shocked by Oren's answer.

"Yes."

Was he the only one who'd been left in the dark? His bitterness leached through to his tone as he said, "Glad to know I was low on everyone else's need-to-know list. How'd you find out?"

"He needed a recommendation from a superior. At the time I was his captain. Don't let it eat at you, son. Neal had secrets that had nothing to do with you. But I'll tell you this...you didn't know Neal as well as you thought. Neal let you see as much as he wanted you to see because I think deep down he loved you and didn't want to see you get hurt."

Matthew felt sick. "Is there something I should know, Oren?"

Oren's mouth tightened, as if he was fighting a battle with himself, and he finally let loose a short exhalation when he'd reached his decision. "No sense in dragging out the secrets of a dead man when he's not around to defend himself. Just suffice to say that Neal would've never made it into the FBI, even if he had passed the psych test."

"What are you talking about?" Matthew asked quietly, suddenly needing to know what had been going on in Neal's life that he'd been totally oblivious to.

"Ah, hell, I should've kept my trap shut," Oren muttered, glancing away. "It ain't my place." Frustration marked the older man's face, deepening the lines around his eyes as his gaze roamed the wild terrain. "I'm just tired of watching you give up your own life because of guilt you feel for a man who really wasn't even in your league."

"I slept with his fiancée," Matthew said. "That's not

exactly something I'm proud of and certainly not something that puts me in some shiny, clean place. We've all made mistakes."

"Neal was about to get fired," Oren stated, turning to look Matthew square in the eyes. "Bad egg. That's what he was behind that shit-eating grin of his. Stop wasting your time feeling anything for that boy. You hear? Kara deserved better. God has a way of sorting things out. By my way of thinking, that's exactly what happened when Neal went out James Dean style. End of story." Oren pushed past Matthew, leaving him to sort out his stunned feelings. He was a few yards ahead of him before he turned and stared in annoyance. "You coming? Or you going to stand there wasting more time?"

Matthew stared after the stocky figure of Oren as he picked his way, surefooted and strong, through the forest ground cover creeping across the path.

Neal? Fired? How could he have missed something like that?

Shaking free of the direction of his thoughts—compelling and disturbing as they were—Matthew hurried to catch up to his partner.

When they finally got to Bernie's house, it was just as empty and deserted as the last time Matthew was there and that sense of foreboding returned. He exchanged a look with Oren.

Oren pulled his weapon and gestured with a short jerk of his head as he whispered, "I'll go check 'round back."

Matthew pulled out his own piece and nodded. Prickles danced along his nape and a discomforting tickle made his guts spasm. He knocked on the front door. "Bernie? It's me, Chief Beauchamp. I need to speak with you. Bernie? You in there?"

No answer. Matthew shook his head—so much for

doing this the easy way—and kicked the door open. It swung free and slammed into the wall, the sound loud and jarring. Still no sign of life. He did a quick check of the two rooms in the shack, and finding them empty, returned outside to find Oren.

He was just clearing the threshold when Oren hollered, "Over here!"

Matthew broke into a sprint in the direction of Oren's voice. He skidded around the corner to see Oren hunkered down beside the dead and mottled body of Bernie Poff.

"Ah, shit," Matthew cursed, holstering his gun and pulling his radio to his mouth to get dispatch on the line. "We've got an 11-44 at Bernie Poff's property. Get Humboldt County Coroner out here ASAP."

"10-4."

Matthew bent down, same as Oren, on the other side of Bernie's body. He swore again. "Looks like he's been out here at least overnight, which means he was likely dead when Kara and I came out here the other day."

Oren agreed, then looked at Matthew, his expression grim. "I think we've got ourselves a problem. This was personal," he said.

"I think you're right. Something tells me Bernie knew more than he should've. Damn old bugger." Regret tasted bitter on his tongue. He was hoping Bernie had nothing to do with this mess. But it would seem at least Bernie wasn't the killer. That was something. Only...the killer had to be someone Bernie knew.

"Whatcha got?" Kara asked, leaning down to peer at D'Marcus's computer screen.

"An architecture student at George Washington University, named Bernice Walz. I saw her name come up on the search but honestly, I looked right past her because she was put away in prison seven years ago for attempting to blow up the Smithsonian when she was just a freshman."

"Talk about ambitious," Zane muttered.

"More like, talk about crazy. Apparently, this chick joined some kind of cult right about the time she got to the college. You know they recruit from the campuses, best way to snag fresh meat."

"Away from home for the first time, needing a friend, they're ripe for the picking, especially someone who has a borderline personality disorder, which I suspect our killer does," Kara murmured, a frown creasing her forehead as memory asserted itself. "Hey, I remember that case. It was pretty big at the time. I was just a field agent but I got lucky and the senior agent pulled me in on some of the action. Mostly just the grunt work—paperwork, gopher activities—but I got to work with some of the best in the bureau. It was quite a coup for a young agent."

"I bet," Zane agreed. "So what do you remember about this Bernice woman?"

Kara searched her memory, that incident nearly forgotten after so much time. "Well, she was certainly bonkers. We never actually caught the mastermind of the plan and she wouldn't turn on whoever was pulling her strings. In fact, it turned out to be pretty anticlimactic. Not that I wanted things to go down in a hail of gunfire but I remember being disappointed on how uneventful her capture was."

"How'd you find her?" Dillon asked.

"Pure luck. We found out that she used to hang out at this café near the Smithsonian. The clerk recognized her picture. Said she was the 'weird chick who stared at the museum for hours.' I think she was waiting for a signal or a sign or something, who knows? We were never really able to unlock that brain of hers. Suffice to say when we caught her inside the museum, she had a bag full of explosives and a note inside her jacket."

"Was it a suicide note?" Dillon asked.

"I don't know. It mostly railed against the establishment, 'the man' and how greed and the love of money can only be eradicated by extreme action."

"So why a museum? Why not a bank?"

"Because this cult believed that the nation's antiquities shouldn't be in the hands of the government. Plus, there was something about the evils of the past being doomed to repeat, yadda yadda…the courts deemed she was nuts and put her into protective custody. I don't think she actually did any time but I thought she'd be locked up for the rest of her life."

D'Marcus looked grim. "Apparently, good behavior goes a lot further than it used to."

A frisson of alarm followed D'Marcus's statement. "What?" she asked.

D'Marcus turned the screen so Kara could read it.

Bernice Walz had been released from St. Elizabeth's Hospital three months ago.

About the same time the first victim went missing.

"Pull the old file on the Smithsonian case. I want to know everything there is to know about Bernice Walz… and find out if there's a connection between her and Bernie Poff."

In the meantime, Kara needed to make a few calls.

Chapter 17

While Kara waited for the right connection to the doctor who had treated and subsequently petitioned for Bernice Walz's release, her thoughts went to Matthew. She wondered what luck he was having at the Poff residence. She hoped he was getting the old codger to come peacefully for questioning. There was no glory in dragging an old man around. Before she could think further on that score, the doctor came on the line.

"This is Dr. Yunez. Can I help you?" Dr. Louis Yunez's voice was thick with an accent and age but not so much that he seemed addled or hard to understand.

"Dr. Yunez, this is Special Agent Kara Thistle with the FBI CARD Team. We're investigating the Babysitter serial murder case and I'd like to ask you a few questions."

"Yes. I saw that case on the news. Terrible business. Anything to help, Agent Thistle."

So far so good. Kara decided the best way to do this

was to jump right in. "We have reason to believe a former patient of yours at St. Elizabeth's may be involved with the case."

"Oh? Which patient?"

"Bernice Walz. Do you recall the details of her case?"

The doctor's long exhalation told her he did. "Of course. Troubled girl at first. Complete mental breakdown after an unfortunate incident that happened shortly after she arrived. For weeks she did nothing but rock herself and sing one of those old nursery songs. Sad story."

"Let me guess…'Pop Goes the Weasel'?" she offered, another piece sliding into place of the mental case that was Bernice.

"Yes, that was the one. I think it was something her mother used to sing to her, perhaps as a child, but well, as I said…sad story."

"Sad how?" She didn't realize being part of a cult was considered fodder for a sob story. "She tried to blow up the Smithsonian."

"Yes. An unfortunate incident. When she came to St. Elizabeth, she was very confused and we often had to restrain her for her own good. Quite violent outbursts at times but after a while she changed and became eager to make amends for what she'd done. You have to remember she was so young when it all happened and she was brainwashed."

Kara didn't believe that for a moment. She'd seen the young woman in action. That chick had had crazy eyes back then; Kara could only imagine what was going through her mind now after spending time in a mental institution. If Bernice turned out to be their suspect, Kara hoped her time spent in St. Elizabeth had been full of electroshock therapy sessions. Pulling her thoughts back from the brink of being unprofessional, she returned to her questioning. "Be that as it may…why was she released? It was my understanding that she'd be in the care of St. Elizabeth's for the rest of her life. I distinctly remember the judge saying she was a danger to herself and others."

"Rehabilitation success." Dr. Yunez sounded dry, as if he didn't actually believe in what he was saying.

"You're telling me that Bernice Walz was somehow cured of her mental illness?" Try as she might, Kara couldn't keep the sarcasm from her voice. She tried again, this time with less snap in her tone. "Please explain. I'm afraid I don't understand."

"Well, she was very young…sometimes, there's a level of success—"

Kara cut in. "Please, doctor. We don't have time for this. There's a child out there, the fourth victim of the Babysitter, who will die if we do not find her before the suspect snuffs out her life. I don't want to hear about statistical data. I want the truth. Why was Bernice Walz discharged?" The long silence was weighted with tension. Kara griped the phone tighter. She was close to screaming. "Dr. Yunez…"

"Budget cuts."

"Excuse me?" That she hadn't been expecting. "How does that affect inmates in state custody?"

"We just don't have the room to house them any longer. We keep the ones deemed psychotic, but those with mild to moderate personality disorders or who haven't exhibited any signs of previous behavior—and I must say Bernice was a model patient—well, the state has authorized the director to rehabilitate and reinstate them into society."

"You just turn these people onto the street?" Her tone was incredulous. Her head was reeling at the ramifications.

Dr. Yunez regained some spirit and he sputtered indignantly. "Of course not. We have several homes purchased as group homes for this very purpose. It's really quite ingenious and forward thinking. We have a very high success rate of positive integration."

"Do you keep a log of these rehabbed people?" Kara tried not to grit her teeth. Damn red tape bullshit. Those people were put there for a reason. *Rehab my ass.* "Please tell me the hospital keeps track of their comings and goings."

"Well, for a time, yes. But…we don't always manage to catch them all. Some slip through the cracks and we assume they've gone to find themselves a better life."

"Or they go on a killing spree," she muttered. "When was the last time Bernice Walz checked in?"

"Oh, let me see here…" The sound of fingers tapping on a keyboard sounded, then Dr. Yunez came back. His tone was moderately flustered. "It seems…"

"She slipped through the cracks?" Kara finished for the doctor.

She heard him swallow. "Yes…it would seem that way," he finished lamely.

"I'll need her complete case file e-mailed to me immediately," she said, and he protested.

"I can't do that without a warrant, you know that Agent Thistle. Patient confidentiality."

Kara didn't have time for this crap. "Are you aware that one of the Babysitter's victims was none other than Senator Nobles's son? This is high profile and people higher up on the food chain want this case closed. There isn't a judge in the state who wouldn't give me a warrant for that information. Have it ready. The warrant will be ready within the hour. Thank you for your help, Dr. Yunez. The federal government appreciates your assistance."

And she hung up. Technically, she shouldn't have been the one making the call. As acting team leader at this point, it should have been Dillon but Kara couldn't stop herself. She felt close. The tension in her gut pushed her to keep going. There was no way she could sit on the sidelines when there was so much at stake. Hopefully, the good doctor didn't start poking around too much. It would be awfully embarrassing if Director Colfax caught wind of her involvement. At that she actually smiled. There was so little joy in her life at this moment…the thought of making that man's head explode was a sweet one and she savored it, even if it was a brief pleasure.

"I've got a bad feeling about this," Matthew said, looking to Oren as the coroner loaded Bernie's body into the rig. It was a miracle the coroner's vehicle was able to maneuver up the mountainside; it wasn't exactly built for off-roading. "Who'd want to kill Bernie Poff? He's got no enemies that I know of. He was basically a harmless old fart."

"Who had a sizable marijuana crop," Oren pointed out.

Sure, there was that, but hell, who didn't in this area? Matthew didn't think his crop had anything to do with his death. No, he was willing to bet his pension that whoever killed Bernie had something to do with the case they were working.

"Bernie got any next of kin?" Matthew asked, rubbing his chin in thought. "I know he doesn't have many friends. Poor old bastard."

Oren shook his head. "Damn shame to die all alone like that. No family that I'm aware…although…" Oren stopped, his face scrunching in thought. His next train of thought came out slowly, as if he weren't entirely sure if his memory could be trusted. "You know...he was married once. Long, long time ago. Damn, I can't even remember her name anymore. Completely forgot about that. Want me to check the county records?"

"Yeah. He owns this property. He's gotta have someone listed as the next of kin."

Briana stiffened. The woman was coming back. She tried to remain still as a mouse, and possibly as small. If she could melt into the wall of the house, she would. Her arms ached from being pulled behind her at an awkward angle for too long and her fingers were numb. She tried wiggling them but it hurt too much to keep at it. Her stomach growled loudly but the woman had stopped feeding her. At this point, Briana would gladly eat that runny oatmeal if only to stop the gnawing pain at the center of her stomach. It felt as if there were a giant rat chomping away at her insides. And she was so thirsty. She'd been given a glass of water early that morning but that'd been all she'd had all day. It was nearly night. Even though Briana was still blindfolded, she could tell by the deepening chill in the air that the sun was going down. The ratty, coarse blanket that smelled like wet dog was all she had against the cold but she didn't dare complain. Briana had a terrible feeling this woman didn't like complainers. Or criers.

Footsteps came closer and although she tried not to, she flinched. A delighted laugh at her reaction made her want to pee herself. This woman was more than mean. She was crazy.

Suddenly, her voice was very close to her ear and Briana turned rigid with fear.

"Ever been on television, *Briana Thistle?*" the voice whispered in her ear. The menace in her voice made

Briana swallow hard but she was too scared to answer. A sharp crack across her cheek made her bite her lip before she cried out. "It's bad manners to ignore someone when they're talking to you," the woman said in an almost gentle manner. "Someone ought to teach you how to behave."

Somehow hearing that soft tone seemed so much scarier.

"I'm sorry," Briana managed to whisper, though how she did it when her throat felt paralyzed with fear she didn't know. "Please don't be mad. I won't do it again," she implored, her voice scratchy and raw from thirst.

That seemed to please her. No more slaps rang sharply against her face and when the woman spoke again, there was a satisfied smile in her voice. "Very nice, Briana. Now…let's get you ready for your big debut. You're going to be *famous*. More so than the rest."

Tears stung Briana's eyes. *Mom…please find me. Pleeeaasse.*

Kara looked up when Matthew walked into the room and immediately knew bad news was coming with him. "What happened?" she asked, thinking the old guy must've put up a fight.

"Bernie's dead."

That got everyone's attention, including Kara's. "How?" she asked.

He shook his head. "Coroner will have official cause of death tomorrow afternoon. But by the looks of the giant hole in his gut I'd say he was plugged with his own shotgun."

"Who'd want to kill that old man?" Kara wondered aloud. He wasn't friendly, to be sure, but around these parts that really wasn't a reason to shut someone up permanently. She looked at Matthew speculatively. "What's your instinct say?"

"It says it ain't no coincidence. I think it has something to do with the case. I think Bernie knew something. Maybe he was getting ready to talk and whoever shot him didn't much like that idea."

"Collect any forensics while you were out there?" she asked.

He sighed and rubbed at his eyes before answering. "Just a few spent shotgun shells and the gun itself," he said.

"Which you say was Bernie's?" Kara asked, and Matthew nodded. So blatant. Like a nice "Screw you" to the authorities. Sounds like their killer.

"Oren's checking on Bernie's next of kin. I guess he was married a long time ago. But I'd say our best lead just got snuffed out."

He sat heavily in the chair by the wall and she was tempted to go over and wrap her arms around his solid shoulders in comfort. She resisted the urge, however, and returned to the group, which had been listening intently.

"Where do we go from here?" Dillon asked, looking to Kara for suggestions. "Bernie getting whacked puts a crimp in our plans to interrogate him."

"You don't say," Kara said dryly. She sank into a chair near Tana and cracked open a bottled water. "Shit," she muttered, her tone as bleak as her sense of hope at this point.

A mild pulse of pain sprang to life at her temples and she reached over to grab her purse. She caught Matthew's gaze as she popped two Excedrin. Their minds seemed to connect and the memory of his ministrations for her earlier headache made her cheeks heat. Her gaze skittered away from his; she was secretly horrified that her hormones

were inappropriately charged and ready to go when it came
to Matthew Beauchamp.

Zane cracked a giant yawn and soon the rest of the
team followed, but no one was going to quit unless Kara
gave the okay for them to seek their beds for a few hours.
She could see their fatigue as easily as she felt her own.
Love and appreciation for her team and their dedication
softened the crazed drill sergeant mom inside of her that
demanded every moment be used to find her daughter and
cut everyone loose for a few hours, seeing as it was nearly
two in the morning already.

"Catch a few winks," Kara said, and it was hard to miss
the looks of relief and guilt that warred with each one.
She clapped Dillon on the shoulder as he moved to the
door. "Don't worry…I get it. Trust me…I get it. But you're
practically falling down. I need you sharp." She caught
each of their gazes. "I need *all of you* sharp to bring her
back home."

Tana's eyes watered and she nodded. "First thing, boss.
You get some sleep, too."

"I'll try," she said, but it was unlikely that she'd get
much shut-eye. Particularly when strange and scary things
tended to happen when she was trying to catch some of
that elusive REM time.

Kara and Matthew walked to her room and the silence
between them felt oddly comforting yet heavy with
expectation. She wanted to invite him in, but for what
purpose? What did she want from him? To talk about the
case? Go over some of her notes to get a fresh perspective?
Grow up, already, she chastised herself as they neared her
door. She craved more than his professional opinion. She
was too tired to dance around the true reason she wanted
him to stay. She craved his solid presence, his arms around
her body, cradling her against whatever might go bump in

the night, she wanted to close her eyes and breathe, as if there wasn't a maniac holding her life in his cruel hands. She wanted to sink into blissful sleep with a man who knew her like no other. The father of her child. Maybe it was time to acknowledge that Matthew had always held a special place in her heart even as she protested that Neal—and only Neal—had the right to trespass.

She turned, her hand on the doorknob, and stared into Matthew's eyes. She whispered one word, laying herself bare and open to rejection, yet instinctively knowing that Matthew would never hurt her.

"Stay."

Chapter 18

Matthew startled at the implication of the request. His feet were willing and after a moment's hesitation he realized his heart was equally willing. Her wide gaze, reflected in cool moonlight, showed vulnerability the likes of which he hadn't seen in Kara since they were kids. The consequence of his acceptance was not lost on him but he couldn't refuse.

Words weren't necessary as he followed her into the cold, dark room. It felt oddly natural to do this, even though it was the farthest thing from natural in either of their lives.

She flicked the small tableside light and the room was bathed in a creamy glow. She went to the mini fridge and pulled out two beers. She handed him his and cracked open hers for a long draught. He did the same as he walked to the edge of the bed and sank to the mattress.

She kicked off her shoes and wiggled her toes with a

satisfied and relieved sigh. She joined him on the bed, sitting close enough that their thighs nearly touched but she didn't look at him. The fact that she started fiddling with the wrapper on her beer bottle gave Matthew cause to wonder if she'd just come to her senses and realized asking him to stay had been a major mistake. He hoped not.

Aside from the sound of beer being swallowed, silence settled between them until she asked, "Is this weird?"

He chuckled, then swigged the last of his beer. "It should be." He swiveled to look at her, demanding her gaze and telling her without words that he wouldn't accept anything but the truth between them at this moment. "But it's not. Not for me, anyway," he added quietly.

She swallowed and glanced down at his lips, then back to his eyes. "Why is that?"

"Because I love you, Kara. Always have and always will," he answered quietly. She inhaled sharply and moisture softened her eyes. A war raged behind those beautiful eyes. The stakes were high and there was bound to be collateral damage if things didn't work out. He knew that. He accepted the challenge.

"Why?" she asked, dropping her gaze to her empty bottle. "I don't deserve your love."

"Don't."

"Don't what?" She rose to throw away her bottle, her back to him. He followed and grasped her arms to make her face him and not the wall. She looked at him and the broken parts inside her called out to him like singing stones. "Don't drag you down with me? I'm a mess, Matthew. Don't you understand? Aside from our daughter, I have nothing to offer you. And if we don't find her in time…" She shuddered at the possibility, her voice dying at the thought. "I'll have even less to offer you…or anyone."

Matthew pulled her into his arms, ignoring the fact that she came reluctantly, and just held her. She smelled of the sea breeze and guns. He grinned at the combination and a chuckle escaped. She pulled away, a frown on her face.

"What's so funny? I'm pouring out my insecurities and you're *laughing?*"

The hurt indignation in her voice sobered him quickly but he took the opportunity to seize her mouth with his before she socked him in the gut or just pulled her gun and plugged him full of holes.

She softened against him, melting into his body, and he fed his hunger for her with deep, tongue thrusts into her hot mouth, coaxing a groan so full of wanting from her throat that he nearly buckled at the knees.

They tumbled to the bed and their kisses became more frenzied and wild. He couldn't get enough of her. His mouth followed wherever his hands roamed and explored; she twisted and arched, her hands buried in his hair or clutching at the bedsheets. A panting moan and whimper, the telltale shake of her knees as an orgasm built to a crescendo in her body—both fueled and buoyed him beyond reasonable thought. All that mattered was this woman under him, giving herself to him in the most primal way possible.

She tensed and her breath caught in her throat, then she exhaled on a guttural cry as she came so hard she could barely breathe. Rock hard and aching, Matthew slowly slid inside her slick heat, gritting his teeth as he tried to go slowly. When she smiled up at him with that sweetly sated expression and then locked her legs around him to drive his cock deeper inside her, he lost all sense of anything but the moment.

And that moment…was so worth it.

* * *

Kara traced a slow imaginary line across the expanse of Matthew's chest as it rose with his slow and steady breathing. So much had changed in so little time yet she couldn't find it in herself to regret their actions. It was as if a piece of herself had broken off and shattered when she'd run away from Lantern Cove and she'd been trying to fix it with little success ever since. But one touch from Matthew and the jagged shards of whatever had broken slowly started to mend.

"What are you thinking?" Matthew asked, the deep rumble of his voice tickling her ear. "Nothing bad, I hope."

"Nothing bad," she assured him, then frowned. "Confusing thoughts...but not necessarily bad ones."

He scooted up the headboard until he was sitting up and Kara was forced to do the same. She withheld a sigh, wondering if she should've been less honest. Sometimes the truth was overrated, she grumbled privately. Especially when feelings could be hurt by careless words or musings. She truly didn't want to heap more misery onto Matthew than she already had, but it seemed that was one thing she excelled at.

"Tell me what you find confusing," he said, his voice gentle. She risked a smile, tempted to lie and smooth everything over, but as he watched her closely, she couldn't give him anything but the naked truth even if it was uncomplimentary or harsh.

"Why are you in my bed? We both know it's not going to work out in the long run. I live in San Francisco, you live here. Neither of us are going to move and I don't have the time or the energy for a long-distance thing. Then, there's Briana...what about her? I know you're going to want to make up for lost time—which I don't begrudge you—but frankly, I can't imagine feeling safe enough to let her out of my sight once this nightmare is over."

"I could come to San Francisco for visits until you feel more comfortable," he suggested.

It was a nice solution, kind and generous even, considering the gas prices right now, but Kara wasn't accustomed to giving someone else consideration when it came to her daughter. She wasn't sure she would adapt well at all to the change, no matter the circumstances.

"And my job…makes it difficult to maintain any kind of relationship," Kara said, drawing a deep breath, hating that she was so logical these days. "So, that brings me back to my original question. What are we doing? Aside from delaying the inevitable?"

He couldn't answer her, which she knew wasn't because he didn't know the answer but because he wasn't willing or ready to acknowledge what she'd already processed. And frankly, she was grateful for his silence. She didn't want to hear that he agreed with her, even if it was the right thing and the most sensible course of action. She lived her life by the dictates of grim reality, but once in a while she just wanted to see life on the other side. The side that didn't peruse crime scene photos over a hastily microwaved dinner, or pay someone else to tuck their child into bed at night, to make sure she said her prayers and brushed her teeth. Yet…she loved her job, so how screwed up was she that she was wasting everyone's time with her crybaby angst routine?

Mood dampened, she moved to get dressed and was startled by Matthew's strong hand catching hers and pulling her down.

"Too much thinking," he said softly, settling her head comfortably under his chin. Her arms wound around his torso as if they were meant to go there. The warmth of his breath played with the hair at her crown. "For tonight... just let it go. I don't have the answers. I don't know how it will work. I just know that I've missed you and I want to enjoy whatever time I have with you."

His declaration stunned her into silence. She remained that way, tucked into his side, for a long while. Then, she started telling the story of their daughter's birth. It was the only thing she could give him at that moment that was honest and pure and beautiful—and should have been his a long time ago.

"Fourteen hours of labor..." he mused when she'd finished.

"*Hard* labor," she added with a nod. "But she came out, screaming at the world. The minute I saw her red little face, all scrunched up and wet, her fists clenched and waving in the air as if she were trying to punch the doctor who delivered her, I fell in love." She twisted to look at Matthew. "She's the most amazing person you'll ever happen to meet," she said, her eyes watering, her voice breaking. "We have to find her."

Matthew pressed a fierce kiss to her lips that lingered as he whispered a solemn vow that she took to her heart as a balm for her battered soul.

"We will."

The next morning, as the team was gulping down scalding coffee and chowing down on powdered doughnuts Matthew had brought to distract everyone from the fact that he and Kara had walked in together, D'Marcus's strangled shout had everyone rushing to his side. He was staring at an mpeg video that started to play when he opened the attachment from an unknown e-mail.

Kara gasped and her knees collapsed as an anguished cry escaped her lips. She hardly noticed Matthew's strong hands catching her, for she stumbled forward, demanding D'Marcus make the screen larger.

A grainy video of Briana, bound hand and foot, blindfolded and gagged, sent quivers of dread and rage spiking through her body. "Oh, baby," she whispered, tears slipping down her cheeks. "Oh, my baby…"

"What the hell is this?" Matthew demanded, his voice strained. Kara shushed him as a singsong voice filled the room from tinny computer speakers.

"'Round and 'round the mulberry bush, the monkey chased the weasel…such a fun nursery rhyme. Don't you agree, Agent *Thistle?* You're probably wondering why I'm doing this…well, if you were smart enough, you'd know. But seeing as you've not figured it out yet…and so many poor little victims have already died on your watch…I don't hold out much hope for this little monkey."

The disembodied female voice was off-camera with the lens focused on Briana, her little body heartbreakingly still as she cocked her head to the side as if she were trying to figure out some way to communicate her whereabouts. Kara wanted to reach out to Briana, touch her, grab her and run out of that dingy room with her.

"I'm so disappointed in you, Kara Thistle. Aren't you supposed to be the best? I beg to differ when I have to leave bigger and bigger bread crumbs for you to follow. What kind of standards are they keeping over at the FBI these days? Can't say I think much of what they consider the best."

There was awful silence and Kara's heart thundered in her chest with pure fear that the killer would do something to Briana on camera but instead, the psycho continued on in a pseudo-sweet tone that set Kara's teeth on edge.

"Be a good girl and say goodbye to your mother, Briana Thistle. Oh, wait, you can't. Your mouth is full of dirty bandana. Oh, well. Life sucks, doesn't it? You know what else sucks? Being misunderstood. Abused by the system. And being locked up. That ranks high on my list of unpleasant. But payback…is *nice*."

And then the video ended.

The woman said "locked up." It *had* to be Bernice Walz. "D'Marcus, find where that e-mail originated," Kara said in a low voice that broke and cracked as panic and fear roiled in her stomach so much that she thought she was going to vomit. "Do it now. Get me a location. NOW."

"I'm on it, boss," D'Marcus said. Vowing in a dark tone, he added, "I'll find it. I swear."

Matthew tried not to pace but his nerves were jangled raw. Seeing his daughter for the first time, tied up like that, nearly sent him to his knees. If he hadn't had to catch Kara, he might've joined her on the floor. He hadn't been prepared for the mental anguish that followed, nor the sense of impotence he felt as the clock ticked with the odds against them.

It seemed a lifetime before D'Marcus had any kind of success. "It's an ISP registered to an Internet café in Garberville," he shouted. A few keystrokes later, he had an address. "At 765 Hoover Lane, a place called Hot Spot."

Kara and Dillon bolted for the door and headed straight for the car until Matthew stopped them. Kara looked at him sharply but he was already on the radio.

"Oren, fire up the bird. We don't have time to drive," he said.

"10-4," Oren answered above the static. "She'll be ready in five."

"You have a plane?" Kara asked.

Matthew shook his head. "Better. A helicopter. More suited for this area. Now, come on. Time's wasting."

They reached the makeshift helo-pad and after a quick exchange, Matthew climbed into the pilot seat.

"You're going to fly this thing?" Dillon asked, eyeing Matthew with clear mistrust. "Are you a licensed pilot?"

"Get in, sweetheart, or get left behind," Matthew bit out as he adjusted his headset. "This bird is leaving in ten seconds."

Kara didn't have the same reservations and climbed in. Dillon, grumbling a bit, climbed in after her.

They took to the sky and what would have taken nearly an hour by car only took minutes by air. Matthew radioed ahead to the Humboldt County Sheriff's Department asking for a car to meet them at the station helo-pad.

Within minutes they were driving to the Hot Spot.

Chapter 19

Kara leapt from the car the minute it pulled into the parking lot, feeling the pressure and the barely contained hope that this was the lead they were hoping for.

She went straight to the counter where a teenaged girl of indeterminate age sat, playing a game of spider solitaire. Kara didn't waste time and immediately flashed her badge, her demeanor hard and determined. The girl straightened and her eyes widened as more officers filed into the small Internet café. Some people, seeing who had entered, decided to make a hasty exit. Kara paid them no heed. She pinned the girl with an intensity that often made people squirm.

"I need to speak to the manager," Kara demanded. She glanced briefly at the girl's name tag, then added with a short-lived smile that was aimed at being disarming but probably ended up looking feral, "Lisa."

"Uh, well, he's not here," Lisa stammered. Her gaze

went from one cop to the next and she swallowed audibly. "Is this about those credit-card receipts that went missing?" Her voice was a mere squeak. "I looked everywhere and I swear, I didn't take anything. I—"

Kara cut her off with a wave of her hand. "We're not here for that. I need to know if there are surveillance cameras installed here."

"Um, I don't think so," Lisa said, chewing her bottom lip. "I could call Big Bob. He's the manager, and he might know."

"Please do. Quickly. And tell him to get down here ASAP."

Lisa scrambled from the stool she was perched upon and disappeared in the back. In the meantime, Kara surveyed the layout of the room while Matthew did the same.

A row of terminals with big flat-screen monitors flanked each wall, with some offering privacy screens. Kara moved straight to the ones with a screen, of which there were only four.

"Whoever this is would've wanted privacy," Kara murmured, turning to Dillon. "Do we know which terminal the ISP belongs to?"

Dillon, who'd had his phone to his ear only seconds ago, closed his phone and shook his head. "But D'Marcus said we can access the information from the terminal. He texted me the numbers."

"Good."

Kara saw Lisa return, a troubled expression on her young face.

"I'm sorry but Big Bob said without a warrant, you can't, uh, well, I guess it's illegal or something to check out the property. I'm sorry," she repeated, clearly uncomfortable with being the one to deliver bad news, especially when

Kara was fairly certain her impatience was evident in her expression.

Matthew stepped forward, saving Kara from what might've been a very bad judgment call. "Lisa, we've got a serious situation here. A child is missing. We can get a warrant if need be but time is of the essence."

"I want to help you out, but Big Bob doesn't like people poking around the computers. And he might fire me if I let you do it without a warrant."

"It's okay. I understand. Don't worry, no one's getting fired today." Matthew smiled, then opened his cell and quickly dialed. Within moments, he was talking to a judge. Kara wanted to kiss him. She should have done that first but she was blinded by a mother's single-minded focus. She mentally berated herself for dropping protocol. Without a warrant, any evidence they may have found wouldn't have been admissible in court. Matthew looked to the girl. "Paperwork is on the way," he said.

"Yesterday a woman came in here to e-mail an attachment. Do you keep a logbook of some sort for users on the terminals?" Kara asked.

Lisa nodded. "But only for the ones who want the privacy screen because most of the other users are gamers and they don't usually care what's going on around them."

"Can I see that logbook?" Kara asked, and the girl hurried to get it. Lisa returned and handed it to her. Kara murmured her thanks and flipped to yesterday's date. She scanned the names, looking for Bernice Walz, but no such luck. No similar name had been put into the logbook. Of course she wouldn't use her name, Kara thought to herself. Her mind moving quickly, she ran through possible pseudonyms the woman might use. She slowly went down the list again, this time looking for anything that popped out at her. Suddenly, something clicked. *Pop.* Goes the weasel. The song used for Jack in the Box toys. The same nursery rhyme that the killer had formed some kind of sick attachment to.

She scanned the list again. Jack Weesle.

"I've found her," Kara breathed, showing Matthew and Dillon. "Terminal 3."

They dusted for prints and managed to pick one up from the mouse but it was only a partial one and smudged at that. Plus the chances that it belonged to Bernice were one in a million considering the kind of traffic a place like the Hot Spot got on an average day. But it was something and Kara was grateful for every lead, however tiny.

They were just finishing up when Kara's phone shrilled to life at her hip. It was Tana.

"We've figured out the connection between Bernie Poff and the suspect...they're related."

Kara frowned. "Related? How?"

"Father and daughter. We missed it the first time around because Bernice used her mother's name and nowhere in her college records is Bernie Poff listed as a relation."

Kara shook her head and whispered to Matthew, "Bernice Walz is Bernie Poff's daughter."

His troubled stare mirrored her own. "We'll be there in a few minutes. We're done here," Kara finished, snapping the phone shut and looking to Matthew. "Fire up that bird. We've got some more ground to cover."

Matthew spoke into the headset as they flew over Garberville. "I've known Bernie for nearly my whole life. I've never heard of him having a daughter," he said.

"Sometimes fathers don't take active roles in their children's lives." The minute the words left Kara's mouth she wished she could take them back. She shot him a quick look to gauge his reaction and nearly held her breath until he seemed willing to let the comment slide. Thank God. She hoped he hadn't drawn parallels to their situation, for heaven knew Matthew would have been an attentive father if she'd given him half the chance. She gulped the lump down that bobbed in her throat and retrained her focus on the case. "Well, D'Marcus is cross-referencing now. This woman had to have had a mother. With some luck, she's still alive."

Less than half an hour later they were back at the motel and yet, they soon hit a dead end. Literally.

"Shit. Nelda Walz died years ago. Natural causes," Zane announced with a sigh.

"Address?"

Zane rechecked the computer screen, then answered, "1917 Crebets Drive, Willits, California."

"That's about two hours from here," Matthew said, and Kara nodded. "Seems she didn't go far for whatever reasons."

"Maybe she wanted to stay relatively close to Bernie for her daughter's sake," Tana suggested. Kara immediately disagreed.

"Then why isn't Bernie listed as the father?"

"Maybe Bernice didn't know who her father was, but that doesn't mean that the mother didn't want to stay close for personal reasons," Tana countered. Kara saw her point. Tana added with a shrug, "People do a lot weirder things for less reason."

"I'm not going to argue with that," Dillon murmured, then clapped his hands and rubbed them together. "I say we get out to this Crebets place and poke around a bit, shall we?"

Kara smiled grimly. "I believe a house call is definitely in order. We'll take two cars. D'Marcus and Zane, you stay here and see what you can scare up on this dead mother. Tana, you and Dillon go together while Matthew and I take the other car." She checked her gun as she reminded them, her chest tight and her heart rate banging a mean drum, "Be careful. We're dealing with a maniac and she has Briana. If you shoot…make it count."

Normally, Kara would never counsel her team in this manner but at that moment, she wasn't Kara Thistle, Special Agent, CARD leader, she was simply a mom bent on getting her baby back—and if she took a pound of flesh with her in the doing, so be it.

Chapter 20

Kara and Matthew pulled up to the house first, with Dillon and Tana close behind.

They exited the car, guns drawn, and started slowly toward the house. It looked like it hadn't been lived in since the old woman croaked, which stood to reason since Bernice, as her next of kin, had been locked up until a few months ago.

Kara gestured with her gun for Dillon and Tana to go right while she and Matthew went left around the house.

Dead silence filled the air as Kara peered around the corner, Matthew at her back. Nothing. No cars, no sign of life inside or out. They did a perimeter check and then converged in the yard.

"No one's here," Tana said in a low tone, disappointment as sharp as everyone else's. "Shit," she muttered, then gestured to Dillon. "Let's go scope out the inside and see if there's anything that will help."

Miraculously, the door was unlocked. The two stepped inside cautiously while Kara and Matthew did a more thorough search of the property.

It was really a dismal place. Apparently, Nelda Walz hadn't cared much for her surroundings. No sign of long-gone flowers in the ancient flowerbeds, just dirt and a few straggly weeds. It was as if even the lowliest of vegetation shunned this place.

The house had a decided lean to it and it was hard to distinguish the storage shed from the main house, they were so similar.

"Can you imagine growing up here?" Kara asked Matthew. "It's sad."

Matthew nodded. "You'd be surprised at how some people allow themselves to live," he said with a grimace, yet his gaze remained sharp. "I'm going to check out the shed."

Kara took in the lush and overgrown landscape that the shack was tucked into and imagined Bernice Walz as a kid, running barefoot like a wild child, dirty nose, and knotted hair with a shrew for a mother. She shook loose the thought. It was a bad idea to let her mind fill in the blanks in the absence of facts, but she couldn't help but try to understand what could create a monster. She thought of the children that had been killed thus far, and as much as she found it distasteful, she placed Briana in the bunch for comparison. What had drawn this crazy woman to her own child? For that matter, what had drawn Bernice to any of the victims? She thought back to when she first met Bernice and remembered what the girl had been screaming when they'd taken her into custody. Kara hadn't thought of that scene in years, but suddenly, it jumped to the forefront of her mind like a shotgun blast from the past.

"Capitalist pigs stealing from the people! Fire is your

only salvation! Let the treasures blow to the heavens!"
The rant was muffled as she was stuffed into the back of
an awaiting federal vehicle but Kara remembered being
struck by the woman's crazed rhetoric. *Fire.* She'd planned
to blow up the Smithsonian. If it hadn't been for her former
professor who'd tipped off the feds when he'd been uneasy
with her increasingly unstable behavior…Kara sucked in
a sharp breath.

She knew the connection!

Kara turned to find Matthew when a hot blast knocked
her off her feet, stunning her stupid for several long minutes
until she got her bearings again. Climbing unsteadily to her
feet, she wiped the dust from her face and eyes, and called
out, her voice hoarse, for Matthew. She heard a moan and
stumbled toward it.

Matthew lay on the ground near the shack, slowly coming to.

"Are you all right?" she cried, her heart pounding a
terrified beat until he nodded that he was okay. She stared
at the ruined house and her stomach pitched. Tana and
Dillon!

"What the hell happened?" he asked, getting to his feet
with Kara's help. He favored his left leg and winced as he
rubbed his knee. Then he saw the damage. "Holy shit,"
he breathed.

They both took off running toward the mess, tears
stinging her eyes as much from the acrid smoke and
smoldering timbers as from the fear that two of her best
friends were dead.

"Be careful," Matthew shouted, grabbing her arm as
she tried to climb into what was left of the house. "It was
obviously rigged to blow, booby-trapped. There might be
others," he warned.

She nodded and carefully made her way to the house.

She rounded the corner and saw both Tana and Dillon had been thrown by the force of the blast through a window. She rushed to their sides, screaming for Matthew.

Blood covered their faces from deep gashes and lacerations. Both were still as the grave. "Noooo," she wailed, going first to Tana to feel for a pulse, then with a sob moved to Dillon. "He's still alive!"

"Tana?" Matthew said after calling in for an ambulance and backup. Kara could only shake her head. Matthew's mouth tightened to a thin line and he swore under his breath. Kara looked away, knowing tears sparkled in her eyes. Tana had been a trusted friend, ally, and co-worker. In some ways she'd been like a sister. A broken sound escaped from her lips before she could stop it and her shoulders shook from the anguish weighing her down. Matthew took her into his arms, heedless of his own injuries, and crooned softly into her ear, though in truth, later she couldn't recall what he'd said. All that registered was that her friend was dead and Matthew was holding her tightly. That was all she could handle at that moment.

Matthew raged silently at the loss of the federal agent. He hadn't known her long or well but in the short time she'd been in his life, he'd gotten the sense that the quiet yet tough-as-nails federal agent had been a good person.

The scene was processed by a different federal team along with the Humboldt County Sheriff Bomb Squad team looking for evidence of more bombs on the property. In the meantime, while the coroner had loaded up Tana's body and an ambulance took Dillon's battered one to the nearest hospital.

"He's going to be all right," Matthew assured Kara when he noted her pale face and stark expression. She turned wide, red-rimmed eyes toward him and he nodded his belief. "That guy's too much a smart-ass to let going through a window slow him down," he said, trying for levity even though the situation was the furthest thing from resembling a comedy.

Her lips trembled with a wan smile and when she pushed a strand of hair from her eyes, her hand shook.

"Hey," he said softly, drawing her away from the chaos around the blasted shell of the house. He looked deep into her eyes, needing her to hear him. "It's not your fault. Don't take this on yourself," he cautioned her with concern. "Please don't. You have enough on your plate. This was the work of a crazy person and everyone who works the job knows the risk. Tana wouldn't want you to do this to yourself."

Kara sucked in a sharp breath and looked away, as if she couldn't bear the truth of his statement, but deep in her heart, she knew he was right. Finally, with a shudder of grief, she looked back at him and just nodded. "I know," she whispered, but her eyes strayed to the scene where Tana lost her life. "But it's hard to believe she's gone."

He cradled her to him and pressed a kiss to her dusty head. "I know, baby," he murmured, feeling her pain as sharply as if it were his own. He knew what she wasn't saying because he was thinking it, as well.

Had the killer set that trap knowing they'd come or had it been set that way for years after Nelda died? And the worst question of all, was Briana's time up now that they were finally closing in?

Matthew tried not to jerk at the thought but it was there. *Heaven help his little girl…*

Briana felt weak from hunger but she did everything she could to make herself blend into the wall she was backed against. The woman hadn't given her any water today.

The cracks from her parched lips made her eyes smart with tears but she held them back. There was something about the woman that had changed. She talked to herself more and sometimes she yelled but as far as Briana could tell, they were alone in the house. But worse than the yelling was the singing. Over and over again, the same song, enough to make Briana want to scream.

"All around the mulberry bush, the monkey chased the weasel…" The singsong voice scared her, and somehow she knew whatever was holding the crazy lady together was quickly unraveling, and that was a bad thing.

Briana cocked her head to listen to the only thing that kept the fear from eating her alive. The soft chirp and whistle of the birds comforted her in some strange way. She didn't know why they were here but their constant song helped her focus on anything but what was happening to her. And they gave her hope.

Her mom would find her. The birds would help her.

It took some doing but Kara locked away her sorrow and grief and regained a fierce and narrowed focus on the case.

"Matthew, before the blast, I think I figured out the connection between Bernice and the victims. If I'm right, it means all this was very personal and not random at all."

"Keep going, I'm listening," Matthew encouraged, a speculative light entering his blue eyes.

"During my first encounter with Bernice Walz, the team was tipped off by her college professor who was disturbed by her increasingly dangerous belief structure. That professor was Robert Garvin."

"The father of the first victim," Matthew surmised. Kara rewarded him with a nod.

"That year was an election year and one particular ambitious senator was looking for reelection. Senator Peter Nobles. Nobles built his platform on tougher sentences for criminal offenders."

"He used the Smithsonian case to further his political gains," Matthew said.

"Right. Of course, it made perfect sense to use that case to his advantage. Bernice was made Public Enemy No. 1 and put away—supposedly for life—in a mental institution. He appealed to the tenderhearted voters out there when he said that considering she was mentally unstable, she was unfit for state prison."

"Bet he's wishing he hadn't gone that route now," Matthew muttered darkly, and Kara didn't disagree.

"Yeah…so, then we come to Hannah Linney…her mother was the district attorney at the time who worked with Nobles to put Bernice away. Even though she wasn't fit to stand trial, the D.A.'s office was hot for a conviction due to the high-profile nature of the case."

"And what's your connection?" Matthew asked.

Kara compressed her mouth to a fine line as she recalled that long-ago case from her past. "I was the agent who helped take her down in the beginning and I was the agent who became the FBI's mouthpiece for this case. In a way…it's full-circle and damn near perfect revenge for that psycho bitch who is bent on repaying the key players who helped thwart her reason for living."

She took a moment to get it together and her shoulders sagged briefly but she was driven by a need to end this and couldn't afford to let anything—fear, grief, rage—throw her off course.

"Let's get back to the motel. I need to let the team

know what's happened and we need to dig a lot deeper into
Bernie Poff's past and figure out where Bernice might be
hiding out. I have a feeling it's probably right under our
noses."

Chapter 21

At the motel, the mood was somber. Kara felt their heartache as deeply as she felt her own.

"Has anyone called Tana's sister?" Zane asked, clearing his throat. "She's the only family Tana had left."

"Yes," Kara said, blinking back the wash of tears that were too close to the surface. "She's on her way up here right now."

"How's Dillon?" D'Marcus asked.

Kara sighed, trying not to let the image of Dillon's bloodied body stay too long in her mind. "They took him to the Southern Humboldt Medical Center where he's listed in critical condition. It's touch and go right now. He was pretty banged up. All we can do is pray he gets better. In the meantime, let's catch this bitch before she finishes out her plan of revenge."

Zane and D'Marcus took a long moment to process their grief so they could temporarily put it aside to do what was necessary. Kara saw the resolve in their stares as they dried their eyes. "What next?"

"I think I've figured out the connections," Kara said, then made short work of explaining the twisted path that Bernice Walz had made since being released early from her incarceration.

"So much for our justice system," Zane said with a low snort. "We do the work and then the politicians let them out again. Sonofabitch," he muttered, and D'Marcus echoed his sentiment.

"Be that as it may, she's out there and our problem again. I say it's about time we take out the trash," Kara said solemnly.

"Amen, sister," D'Marcus said, his gaze narrowing. "I'm on it," he declared, swiveling in his chair, fingers flying over the keyboard as he accessed every database known to man searching for everything and anything they could find on Bernie Poff.

It wasn't long before D'Marcus got a hit.

"I think the problem may have started with dear old ma," D'Marcus stated derisively. "I've got an old social services file on her regarding Bernice. Seems mental instability runs in the family. Apparently, Nelda was part of some radical militia group in the '60s but she managed to get away before the hammer came down. The key players went to prison, except one."

"Who was the one who got away?" Matthew asked, not quite sure he wanted to know the answer.

"Your friend, Bernie."

"Damn," Matthew swore, hardly able to believe it, but it sure explained why Bernie had seemed to hate law enforcement. "But he was never a problem," Matthew said, having a hard time grasping that straw. but it was hard to hold on to that with the evidence staring him in the face. "Guess it goes to show you never truly know a person."

"To be fair, you can't really say you *knew* him," Kara reminded him softly. "He saved your life and you had a soft spot for him because of it but other than that, what did you know of him? He didn't seem the sort to keep an open book on his life."

"You got me there," Matthew acknowledged, but he felt a loss at the newfound information. "I liked him," he admitted. "I appreciated his simple philosophies, those that he chose to share with me, that is."

Kara's expression was understanding but she was ready to move forward. "What else you got, D'Marcus?" she asked anxiously.

"I think that explains why she didn't list Bernie as the father. She probably wanted to distance herself and her daughter from the stigma Bernie might carry if anyone found out about his involvement with the militant gang."

"It doesn't explain why she went nuts," Zane said wryly.

Kara chewed her bottom lip. "You're right. We've still got a missing piece. Keep looking, D'Marcus," she directed, then turned to Matthew. "Aside from the main house, were there any other homes or cottages up on Bernie's property?" she asked.

Matthew thought about it, then answered. "I think he had an old one-room shack that he used when he stayed in the mines too late. Why? What are you thinking?"

Kara shook her head. "I don't know…but I think we have to go back. There's something about that place that gives me the creeps, but I can't get it out of my head that we've missed something."

"If you feel that way, I say we should listen to your instincts. You haven't been wrong yet," Matthew said, willing to put his faith in her when it counted the most. "Let's go take another look."

Kara grabbed her jacket and left instructions with Zane and D'Marcus to call if anything else was found or if they received word about Dillon, then she and Matthew hit the road.

They pulled up to the old house where Bernie had spent his adult life and Kara couldn't shake the feeling that someone was walking over their graves. Her skin crawled and there was a sense of foreboding that rode her spine. She didn't know if it was because of that hallucination she last saw here or the fact that Bernie had died on this mountain.

"You okay?" Matthew asked, noting her rigid posture as they trudged up the trail.

"Not really," she answered in spite of herself. She risked a crooked smile and Matthew returned it. Somehow that easy connection between them made her feel better. That was something to be marveled at because there was nothing about the situation that could be described as anything less than stressful. "Matthew...I've missed you in my life," she admitted.

He stopped. They held each other's gaze for just a heart-beat but it could have been an eternity for what it conveyed. He canted his head at her. "So what are we going to do about that?" he asked, his smile somewhat pained.

She offered a heavy and disconsolate sigh. "Not a clue. Certainly not something I could figure out this second but I felt the need to tell you that. There's been so much between us, both in the past and the present, that I felt I owed it to you to be honest."

His gaze was grave as he said, "I appreciate that."

"But I don't know what will happen when this is all

over," she said, swallowing hard to get the words out. "I can't say I can be the woman you need me to be or even the woman I would like to be. I'm not the woman you remember and I doubt I ever could be again."

There was something so incredibly sad in his gaze that it took nearly everything in her not to look away. It was too powerful and stark, as if he were drinking in her appearance and tasting her soul with one lingering sweep of those azure eyes. If wishes were like raindrops she'd take each and every one to wish that life had dealt different hands to them all. But that wasn't possible and what was done could not be undone. Tana was gone. Dillon was hanging on to his life with his fingertips and her—their— daughter may already be gone. Tears stung her eyes and Matthew knew it was time to push on because he hated to let people see her cry.

It was a considerable hike to where Bernie's miner's shack was located. It was near enough to the mine and Kara was surprised she hadn't seen it the last time they ventured this far. But then, she'd nearly been ready to jump out of her skin that other time so she cut herself some slack. As they approached, an odd sound came to them from the distance.

She cocked her head to the side. "Do I hear…birds?"

Matthew nodded. "Bernie kept canaries," he answered.

"Canaries?"

"The miners used to take canaries down into the coal mines with them because canaries are especially sensitive to methane and carbon monoxide. So if the bird stopped singing and keeled over, the miners knew they'd better clear out of there or else they'd be as dead as the bird."

Kara raised a dubious brow. "I thought Bernie was mining for long-lost treasure, not coal."

Matthew shrugged. "He was. But he was also digging around in a mountainside where there was very little ventilation. He wasn't going to take the chance."

"Or maybe he just liked birds and used the old miner lore as an excuse to keep the birds around," she teased, eliciting a soft chuckle from Matthew.

"You might be right. But we should probably take the birds back down with us. It's cruel to leave them out here with Bernie gone."

Kara agreed but as they neared the shack, suddenly Kara felt cold all over, as if someone had just plunged her entire body into a vat of liquid nitrogen. She froze and fear tickled her senses. She drew her gun, prompting Matthew to do the same. He looked at her inquiringly but held his position.

She didn't know how to tell him but she knew something bad was about to happen. She gestured silently toward the shack and they flanked the small building.

Kara inched toward a window opening and slowly peered inside. The shabby contents included a faded and dingy sofa with stuffing spilling from its ruptured sides, and a rickety end table with gun magazines littered across its top. A narrow hallway to the one bedroom met her gaze. She caught movement and ducked down but not before catching a glimpse of something that stopped her heart.

The still and bound form of her daughter being tugged down the hall as if she were deadweight made Kara want to run screaming into the shack to pump bullets into her tormentor's body. Her heart cried out and her hands shook as fear gripped her at the sight of Briana's motionless and silent frame. Why wasn't she struggling? Fighting? Trying to get free? *Oh, baby, please don't be dead. I'm here, baby girl!* Swallowing hard and blinking back tears of panic, she compartmentalized her feelings as if that little girl lying on the grubby floor was not her heart and soul but a stranger's child that she was trying to save. The thought narrowed her focus to a pinprick. She motioned to Matthew as he crept along the side that she was going in and she needed cover.

He jerked his head at her, frowning at her decision, but she was moving before he could persuade her to go a different route.

Kara slid into the house, keeping her back to the wall and her eyes trained for any hint of movement. She tried not to look at Briana while the danger was still high. First take out the threat; then check the hostage. Doing it the other way around got people killed.

Kara pressed her back against the wall and listened for any sound. She could hear someone muttering in the bathroom. The door opened with an angry squeal of resisting hinges and then slammed shut. The footsteps stopped and sweat popped along Kara's forehead as her grip tightened on her gun. The footsteps resumed, then Kara saw Bernice Walz clear the hallway. Kara cracked her in the face with her elbow, hard enough to send a spray of blood from a busted nose to paint the wall behind her. Kara whirled on the woman, ready to take her down at gunpoint, but Bernice had rallied faster than Kara expected and surprised her with a vicious kick to the gut. As she doubled over and gasped for breath, Bernice went to send Kara's teeth into the back of her throat with the heel of her boot, but Kara saw it coming and managed to roll to the side, avoiding the hit. She scrambled to her feet, her stomach roiling with the need to puke, but she refused her body's need. Instead, she smiled at the woman who was regarding her with a nasty grin tainted red by the bloody snot running from her nose.

"Took you long enough. Didn't I leave enough bread

crumbs for you to find?" Bernice taunted. Kara fought to keep from riddling her with bullets. Bernice wiped her nose with the back of her hand and flung the viscous mass to the floor. "I expected better of Special Agent Kara Thistle," she mocked.

"Bernice Walz, you have the right to remain silent," Kara said from between gritted teeth, the desire to end this right now so strong it took every ounce of training to stay cool.

"Aren't you wondering why? I bet it's eating you up inside." Bernice moved slowly and Kara leveled the gun at her head. She held her hands up in surrender. "So touchy."

"Matthew...is Briana okay?" she called out, never once letting her gaze falter from Bernice. "Matthew?" her voice rang shrilly as her fear ate at her.

"I highly doubt that," Bernice said sadly. "The dose of tranquilizer I gave her could've killed a horse. You can imagine how quickly it would work on a small, defenseless girl." Bernice tsked and shook her head in sympathy. "So close yet...well, you know the saying."

Kara's heart contracted and tears blinded her. It was the slip in concentration Bernice needed and she sprang like a mountain cat on its quarry, deadly and accurate. Bernice knocked Kara to the ground and the gun went spinning out of reach. With Bernice's weight on her she couldn't scramble to a better position. Nails raked down her face as Bernice tried to squeeze her eyeballs out. Bernice matched her in size and weight, but Kara wasn't above playing dirty to gain an advantage. Breaking free, she grabbed a breast and twisted so hard she wouldn't have been surprised if she tore flesh. The woman howled and tried jerking away. Kara used this opportunity to roll them both until Kara was on top. She wasted little time in clocking the bitch twice before Bernice bucked and Kara went crashing to the floor. This time they both scrambled for the gun. Kara knew if she didn't get her hands on it first, they all were going to die. An extra spurt of adrenaline pumped through her muscles and she managed to get her fingers curled around cold metal just in time to put the muzzle of her Glock right smack against Bernice's sweaty forehead. "That's right, bitch. Back the hell off before I blow your face to kingdom come," Kara growled, getting to her feet slowly. Bernice wavered, indecision in her gaze, then the confidence returned.

"Such a good little agent," she said, catching her breath. "I heard there was an accident. How many did my little present take out?"

"Why'd you do it?" Kara asked, ignoring Bernice's taunting question. "Do you even have a reason or are you just bat-shit crazy for the hell of it? Like mother like daughter, perhaps?"

Bernice's gaze narrowed. "Watch it, government girl. There's more to this story and if you don't play nice, I won't tell."

Kara smirked. "You're wrong. The story ends here. You go to prison where you should've ended up years ago instead of the loony bin, though I'm sure those years were well spent."

Something flashed in Bernice's eyes as her nostrils flared with hatred. Kara shook her head in disgust. "You're pathetic and your inane attachment to that creepy nursery rhyme isn't clever or metaphoric as you tried to make us believe. You're just crazy. It's all documented in your file from St. Elizabeth's. *Psychotic break* sound familiar? Just your run-of-the-mill nut job."

"Kara!" Matthew's frightened voice chilled her to the

bone. "Briana's in bad shape! Her breathing is shallow and her heartbeat is weak!"

Bernice's stare shifted to where Matthew and Briana were and her lips twisted in a macabre smile. "Uh-oh. Methinks time ran out for little Briana Thistle. The ambulance will never get here in time," she commented almost conversationally. Then Bernice's expression went from happy to venomous and she nearly spat the words when she said, "How does it feel to lose something precious?"

Not expecting the sudden attack, Kara swallowed her revulsion and tightened her grip on the gun. "You're a monster. A sick freak who they should've kept locked away in a dark hole for the rest of your miserable life," Kara whispered, refusing to let her tears blind her this time. "They're just babies. What made you so awful?" she asked, though she hadn't expected an answer. When Bernice gave one, Kara found herself listening in stunned silence.

"I was pregnant," she hissed, her eyes flashing with loathing so hot Kara nearly stumbled back for fear of getting burned. "I lost my baby in that mental hospital that you helped put me in and I swore every single person who had a hand in taking my baby would pay with their own."

"There's nothing in your file that states you were pregnant," Kara said stiffly. "You're lying."

"Of course it's not in my file," Bernice scoffed. "That weak dick politician Nobles didn't want any bad press to taint his election chances. There was an *unfortunate accident* and my baby was thrown out with the trash. I was beaten nearly to death by one of the orderlies but Nobles made sure that report never saw the light of day. All it says in my file is that I was prone to violent outbursts and appropriate *measures* were taken. You can read between the lines and guess what kind of treatment I was subjected to."

Was it true? And if it was, why hadn't Dr. Yunez mentioned the miscarriage? She thought of Senator Nobles and it made her sick to realize that what Bernice was saying was possible. Nobles had been single-minded in his pursuit. He would've made sure anything with the power of sullying his campaign went away. Including inconveniently pregnant radicals. "I'm sorry you lost a child," Kara said yet secretly horrified at the thought of this woman being a mother. It was tragic how it happened but perhaps it was a blessing in disguise. "But you're the one who put your child in danger when you tried to blow up the Smithsonian. I was just doing my job."

"Oh, I know all about you and your work ethic," Bernice sneered. "Kara Thistle, the hotshot darling who could do no wrong. You made quite a name for yourself at my expense."

"I wasn't in charge of your case," Kara corrected from between clenched teeth. "It's not my fault they chose me out of a hundred other agents who could've done just as good a job on that case!"

"But it *was* you. Lucky you. With your perfect face and perfect body...everything about you is just *perfect,* isn't it?"

Kara refused to be drawn into an argument centered on vanity. She couldn't help what she looked like any more than Bernice could help what she looked like.

For a moment, Bernice seemed lost in a spasm of grief but it was gone in a flash, just as her moments of lucidity came and went.

"My baby was all I had. And you helped take it from me. But now you feel the heartache, the rage, and I revel in it. Do you hear me? I *revel* in it!"

"You killed your father because he knew it was you, didn't you?"

Bernice spat. "Meddling old man. A little too late to play daddy at this late stage in the game, don't you think? Besides, he was going to tell the local yokel chief of police and I didn't want to deal with the complication. But he made for a nice clue to leave behind."

"So this is your grand finale? This showdown between me and you? This was what you killed all those innocent children for?" Kara asked, but as the words left her mouth she felt that cold prickle at the back of her neck again. Bernice offered a jackal's grin and Kara backed away but kept her gun trained on Bernice. Kara's look of disgust was plain on her face as she said, "You're going to prison so you can't hurt anyone else. Ever again."

Bernice laughed, the sound sending ice splintering through Kara's body. Then the woman pulled a small hand-held device from her pocket. "Sorry to disappoint you but I have no plans to go to prison. I'm not one for small, enclosed spaces. Given my history, I'm sure you understand. Any last words?" she asked, a grim smile on her face.

Kara's breath stopped and she knew she was looking at a detonator. She was going to blow them all to hell along with her. "You don't have to do this," Kara said, stalling for a miracle. "You need help. You weren't always like this, right? Remember when you had hopes and dreams, goals?" Her mind searched for a possible weak spot in the fabric of Bernice's mind, something she could use to her advantage. "When you were a freshman...an architecture student. You were the top of your class...you don't have to waste all that potential on death and destruction. Your mom moved you away from your dad and that militia gang to give you a better life. Is this how you repay her for that?"

"My mother is dead, therefore your statement is immaterial, but just for the sake of arguing, if my mother were alive, no doubt she'd be very proud. Before she went soft, she was a radical liberal who believed in something. Just like I believed in something and paid the ultimate price. Now you too will pay for doing what you feel is right. Your drive to catch the bad guy has landed you here, with me. *Brav-o,*" Bernice said, gesturing with the device. She narrowed her gaze. "Did you forget? I'm smarter than you. By about fifty IQ points. Your attempt at getting inside my head is pathetic. Just like your investigating skills. This is the end of the story and I get to choose how we all say goodbye."

"The hell you do," Kara muttered before taking a wild chance and plugging a single shot straight through Bernice's brain.

Bernice's body fell to the ground in a heap and Kara let out a shuddering breath as the device rolled harmlessly from Bernice's dead fingers to stop against the leg of the end table. "*The end,* you psycho bitch," she whispered, taking one last look at the woman who had wrecked so many lives. Turning away, she ran to where Matthew cradled Briana in his arms.

The terrified look in his eyes surely mirrored her own. "Is she?" she couldn't say the words. They stuck in her throat like dried, day-old bread. Tears flooded her eyes. "Please say she's still alive. I can't take it if she's not."

"Barely. Air support should be here in two minutes." Matthew looked at her through a veil of his own tears.

Kara choked down a wave of relief and fell to her knees

beside her baby girl. Together they held Briana, willing their strength into her small body until they heard the whir of a helicopter landing outside.

Chapter 22

It was several days before Kara felt safe enough to leave Briana's hospital bed. Briana suffered from dehydration, and her arms and legs were severely chafed from the rope. The drug Bernice had injected her with had nearly stopped her heart but Briana was a fighter and her heart had stubbornly refused to stop beating, even if the drug had made the effort sluggish. As a precaution, the doctors had suggested Briana stay in the hospital until they were certain the drug had completely passed from her system.

Kara rose and placed a soft kiss on her daughter's forehead as she slept. She looked up to see Matthew standing in the doorway, watching them. She felt heat tingle in her cheeks as she rose and walked toward him.

"She's asleep," Kara said quietly, gesturing that they step outside the room. Matthew agreed though she could see the uncertainty in his gaze as they stepped over the threshold and into the bustling hospital hallway. Kara crossed her arms and rocked on her heels a bit, then said, "She seems a different kid lying in the bed. She looks older, more mature. I'd give anything to have her go back to seeing the world as a child does, full of wonder and possibility. Now there are shadows in her eyes that I can't take away."

"She's a strong girl," Matthew said, but she knew he shared her sadness at their daughter's loss of innocence. "She'll get through this. It's a blessing she's alive. Everything else falls by the wayside when you put it into perspective."

"I know...it's still hard." Kara swallowed, then tackled another painful subject. "We're leaving soon. The team cleared out this morning and as soon as Briana is given the okay by her doctor, we're going to head back home to San Francisco."

Matthew was silent for a moment. She stiffened as any number of defensive comments flew to mind as she prepared to launch a tactical assault in response to what she knew was going to be a fight against her decision, However, when it didn't come, she felt simply deflated. "Matthew? What are you thinking?"

His hands gravitated to his hips and a slow sigh whistled from his mouth as he answered, his voice full of disappointment that he couldn't put words to. "You have to do what you feel is right. But so do I."

"What does that mean?"

"Kara, what do you think it means? She's my daughter, too. I've missed out on enough of her life. I don't plan to miss any more."

A pang of heartbreak made it difficult to speak so she nodded instead. "I understand. I guess we'll work out a visitation arrangement. Weekends might be hard to arrange with my schedule but maybe a few times a month or maybe during summer vacation…" Her voice trailed as his look darkened and she knew this was a tragic situation that was never going to get easier. But what did he expect? She wasn't about to give up her job for his convenience. If she wouldn't do it for Neal…she swallowed hard…then she wouldn't do it for Matthew, either. "We'll figure something out," she said hoarsely, then turned on her heel, eager to get away before she made a complete fool of herself.

"Kara…"

She was tempted to keep walking. Already tears were too close for comfort and she had plenty to do before Briana was discharged. But she turned stiffly, giving him at least that because she felt he'd earned it. "Yes?"

He crossed to her with long, purposeful strides and her heart quailed and fluttered like one of Bernie's canaries stuck in a cage with a predator. But she held her ground, staring him down, daring him to take what he wanted and leave no prisoners, least of all herself.

His arm encircled her waist and pulled her roughly to him, his gaze devouring her with the intensity of a man who knew love and wasn't afraid to grab it with both hands. His lips touched hers, kindling a fire deep inside her that burned and ravaged and made her want to run, and his words blistered her heart in the most unkind way.

"Briana's not the only one I want in my life."

She made to protest but it was weak and easily silenced as he whispered against her lips, "The choices we make follow us forever, dogging our steps until they catch up and brand us with their mark. The question is…what mark are you willing to bear for the rest of your life? I know my answer. Do you know yours?"

He inhaled her scent, eyes closed, and brushed his lips across hers one final time. Then he walked away.

* * *

Walking away was nearly as painful as it had been watching Briana struggle to breathe. But he knew Kara wasn't ready to stay and he wasn't ready to go unless she was going to embrace everything that it meant to be together. He wasn't satisfied with stolen moments in each other's bed, nor did he relish the idea of seeing his daughter once in a while when Kara found the time to meet him halfway for visitation. But he also knew that if he pushed, Kara would bolt. It was her M.O., her way of dealing with thoughts and feelings that scared her or made her feel uncertain. A control freak to the nth degree, she was as stubborn as she was beautiful. And he loved her. Bone-deep, gut-wrenching, holy-shit-I'd-die-without-her kind of love. And he'd waited this long, he supposed he could wait a little while longer for her to come around. And if she didn't? Hell, he'd cross that bridge when he came to it.

Briana stared at the angry red welts on her wrists and slowly rotated them to ease the stiffness.

"Does it still hurt, baby?" Kara asked, concern chasing away the fatigue born from sleeping at her daughter's bedside. "Should I call the nurse for some Tylenol?"

Briana shook her head, her eyes faraway and troubled. Kara ached to take away the pain, but she couldn't, and the inability to ease her daughter's heartache made her feel useless.

"I miss Mai." Briana's voice came out a croak as a tear leaked down her face.

"I know, sweetheart. I do, too," Kara said, wiping away the tear gently and pushing a lock of hair from Briana's face. "She loved you very much. And I know she misses you, too, wherever she is."

"Is she going to come back as someone or something else?" Briana asked.

Kara considered her answer, not quite sure how to respond. She'd never had time for church and although she knew Mai had been a practicing Buddhist, she was unfamiliar with the ins and outs of her religion. However, Briana's question told Kara that Mai had shared her beliefs with her daughter. The knowledge made her realize she'd missed out on more of Briana's life than a few dance recitals and homemade dinners. "Um, what do you feel in your heart?" Kara asked, fighting tears.

Briana thought about it, then nodded slowly. "I think she would've wanted to come back as a bird," Briana said softly. "She said birds were lucky because they could fly away from trouble if they needed to and they brought beautiful music into the world." Briana nodded, mostly to herself. "Yes, she'd definitely come back as a bird."

"Then you're probably right."

Briana was quiet for a long moment and Kara thought maybe she was tired so she prepared to leave her alone for a few minutes to go to the cafeteria for a bite. But Briana's words stopped her.

"Mom…can we take the birds home with us?" she asked in a small voice.

"Birds?" Kara repeated, frowning. "What birds?"

"The birds that were at that place where the bad woman kept me."

"The canaries? Why?" Kara was puzzled.

"They kept me company," she whispered, and Kara nearly cried for the pain in her daughter's voice. "The sound of their singing…it reminded me of Mai. And I thought maybe one of them was Mai…looking out for me."

Kara's heart was seized in a fierce grip as she nodded.

"Of course we can, baby girl," she answered, blinking against the moisture flowing from her eyes. "We'll take them all."

Chapter 23

It was the second time Matthew and Kara had worked out a visitation. This time Kara had traveled to Lantern Cove instead of meeting Matthew halfway. Briana was warming to him, although she was still reserved. Not that he blamed her. It was a lot to take in after such traumatic circumstances. But today, he had a present for her.

"I heard you were interested in taking guitar lessons," Matthew said conversationally as he walked to his truck to retrieve her present. She trailed after him. "Did your mom tell you I started playing guitar when I was about your age?"

He glanced back at Briana and she nodded shyly. "She said you were really good."

"She did, did she?" Matthew asked, sending a playful look Kara's way, which she responded to with a blush.

"I may have said you weren't *terrible*," Kara said.

"High praise." Matthew grinned.

He opened the truck door and pulled a Yamaha three-quarter size guitar, perfect for her small frame, from the truck and handed it to her. She gasped as she took the guitar gingerly into her hands and stared in delight. She turned to Kara. "Look what Matthew got me!"

He winced ruefully at the fact that she still didn't feel ready to call him Dad but he was a patient man; he could wait. "What do you think?" he asked. "Think you can handle lessons on that baby?"

"I think so," she answered, beaming at him. "Can I start now?"

"Sure, but wait," he said, producing a pick from his pocket. "You might want to use this until your fingers get used to the strings."

"Thanks!" She bounded off to sit in the sand where she could strum some experimental sounds.

"You'll spoil her," Kara said lightly.

"I mean to," Matthew returned with a slight twist of his lips. "I've got a lot of catching up to do. Is it too early to buy her a car?"

Kara gasped and gave him a mock punch in the shoulder. "You better not buy her a car or I will shoot you. I don't even want to think of Briana behind the wheel for a very long time."

"Me, neither," Matthew said. "I want to savor every moment and draw each one out for as long as possible. Plus, I need to start saving for her college fund. She might have to wait on the wheels just yet."

"Amen to that."

They walked in silence together, enjoying the brisk air of the beachside park, and listened as the waves crashed on the shore. "How's that pretty-boy Brit of yours doing?" Matthew asked casually, though he was truly concerned. The man had earned his respect, but Matthew would never admit it openly. Kara seemed to know this and smirked as she answered.

"He's doing fine. Aside from a small scar on his cheek that he says makes him look dangerous, he's good as new and just as much of a pain in the ass as he was before."

"Well, I suppose it's too much to hope that he might've lost those pretty-boy good looks through all this," Matthew said half-seriously. "I mean, put a dress on the guy and he'd pass for—"

"A very odd-looking woman," Kara finished, eliciting a laugh from Matthew.

"You're right." Matthew sighed. "Maybe he's not that pretty."

"I'll pass along the sentiment," Kara said dryly. "I'm sure Dillon would be flattered to know you're not attracted to him. I think he said he was worried for a while but to tell you that he doesn't swing that way. Ever."

"Neither do I," Matthew growled. They sat beside each other on the flat side of a play structure and Matthew drew a deep breath, as he prepared to speak. He'd rehearsed his speech a million times as he'd lain awake in bed since Kara and Briana left Lantern Cove weeks ago.

"What if I moved to San Francisco?" he blurted out. *So much for finesse.* Kara's startled expression prompted the rush of words that followed. "I want to be with you and Briana. I know you have feelings for me, beyond friendship, and I've had feelings for you since we were kids. I want to build a family for Briana, but I don't want you to feel that you have to give up your life to come back to Lantern Cove so…I've put in an application for the San Francisco Police Department." Kara's look of dismay nearly killed his nerve to continue but he was already knee-deep in it and there was no sense in pulling back now. "I know I'm older than most new officers but I think with my experience I could be an asset to any department," he said gruffly, betraying his insecurity about tearing up his roots and starting at the bottom with a new department. But he was willing to do it for Briana and Kara if only she'd say the word.

"I can't ask you to do that," Kara said, the light in her eyes dimming. "It's not fair to you."

"Let me be the judge of what's fair when it comes to my career. I want to do this. I want you and Briana close. I'm not saying we have to live together because I know we're not at that place yet. But I know what I want and you two are it."

"Matthew...I could never—"

"It's my choice."

"You're only doing it because of us. Your life is here. We'll make it work with Briana. As far as you and I..." She shook her head and his hopes plummeted. "I told you, I'm not the person you remember. And maybe I don't want to be."

Matthew drew closer and just the scent of her skin, light and fragrant as a sunny day, made him ache for everything that was just out of his reach. When he spoke, his voice broke with the emotion he was trying to hold inside. "That day at the hospital I asked you what mark you wanted to wear for the rest of your life. Did you ever figure out what that was?"

Kara shook her head in dejected silence.

"I know my answer. I want to wear the mark of happiness. You and Briana represent everything that's good and worth having in my life. It's not this place or my job. My home is wherever the two of you are. So, the ball is in your court. When you figure things out, I'll be waiting."

Kara looked torn. He knew that feeling. He'd been through it all the years when they were kids and Neal was the one she looked at with love and adoration. Now that he knew how he felt in his own heart, he no longer knew conflict of that nature. He offered her a pained, yet somewhat playful grin, and went off to play with Briana, leaving Kara to her turbulent thoughts.

It was late that night when Kara was tucking Briana into bed, exhausted after the long drive back to the Bay Area, when she was surprised by Briana's sleepy question.

"Do you love Matthew?"

Kara startled, all thoughts of sleep and a sore back from sitting in one position too long gone in an instant. "What do you mean, sweetheart?"

"I dunno. I mean, you look at him funny and he looks at you just as funny. I thought maybe that's what moms and dads look like when they're in love. And if you're both in love…how come you live apart?"

"That's a lot of complicated questions for such a late night, kiddo," Kara said, wondering how to answer. Should she offer the truth? Or lie to keep her feelings private because she wasn't ready to admit them to herself?

She sighed, and with that one small sound, she betrayed herself. Briana looked at her and said, "If you wanted us to move to Lantern Cove, that would be okay with me."

Kara stared, surprised at the quiet sadness in her daughter's gaze. "Why, honey?"

Briana rubbed at her nose before answering. "It's hard being here without Mai. Everywhere I look, she's there but not really. I think it might be easier to be somewhere she's never been."

Kara was floored by her daughter's keen maturity, but the cause of it pained her deeply. She pushed a lock of hair from her eyes. "But wouldn't Lantern Cove bring up bad memories? I mean…your time there wasn't exactly a picnic."

"Yeah, but Matthew is there. He makes it all right."

Kara waited to feel jealousy at her daughter's innocent comment but it didn't come. Instead, she felt warm and teary-eyed that Briana considered Matthew her champion.

"Yeah, he does, doesn't he…" she murmured, smoothing a knuckle down the soft fuzz of her daughter's cheek. She pictured leaving the city behind and living by the beach, watching as Briana adjusted to a quieter pace, strumming the guitar by the bonfire with Matthew…and smiled.

Always Matthew. Strong, reserved Matthew. So many years lost in regret…she thought of Neal and how she carried the guilt of his death around with her, wondering how things might've been different if she'd stayed.

Now she knew it wouldn't have been better. Neal was of weak character, always covering his flaws with jokes and charisma. Being around Matthew would have illuminated her true heart's desire and it would have destroyed Neal just the same when he realized he'd lost her. Tragedy would have struck either way.

Kara took a long look around her small house and knew Briana was right.

They couldn't return to the present and look to the future without the ghosts of the past lurking around every corner.

She never thought the day would come that she'd be ready to let her career take a backseat to her personal life but now that she was considering it…the idea didn't fill her with panic like she thought it would.

The truth was, this case had changed her. And she didn't know if she could go back to the way she was before.

Crossing to her cell phone, she called Dillon.

"Someone better be in grave danger," Dillon snapped,

sleep making his tone gravelly and hoarse. "Or better yet, dead, otherwise you're in a heap of trouble, Thistle."

Kara chuckled and realized Dillon would be the hardest to let go of. "I'm going to put in for a transfer. I wanted you to know first," she said.

The sleepiness left his voice. She half expected him to give her a ration of shit over her decision but he didn't. Instead, she heard respect. "It's about time you did something right for yourself," he said. Then, he added, "He's a good man. A lucky one, too."

Kara grinned. "Actually...I think I'm the lucky one."

"Go get your man, Agent Thistle."

She laughed and clicked off. That was one bit of advice she didn't mind following. Not one bit.

Epilogue

Several months later

Kara stood at her kitchen window and took a deep lungful of the salty sea air, sharp and tasting of rain as another spring storm hovered on the horizon, and a smile born of happiness and gratitude curved her lips.

Two strong arms slid around her torso as firm lips nuzzled the soft skin of her neck. She angled into Matthew's body for better access.

"No regrets?" Matthew pulled away and she turned to him, the smile remaining.

"None," she answered, looking into his eyes. "I love it here. Feels different from before, when I was younger. For the first time I feel at peace. Is that weird? I mean, I never thought Lantern Cove would make me feel at rest. With my dad, Neal and then the Babysitter case…it seemed

Lantern Cove would always harbor bad memories. Until you. And Briana."

He planted a light kiss on her mouth and she leaned into him, ever hungry for his touch, his warmth. "And soon..." he said, his voice trailing softly.

She blushed and her hand strayed to her still-flat stomach. A rush of love made her extremities tingle... or was it the memory of what put that little tadpole in her tummy that made her feel that way? She smothered a giggle and pressed another kiss to his lips. "Soon, everyone in town will know what we've been up to."

He grinned against her mouth and his hand slid to her rear for a gentle squeeze. "Good. I want the world to know Kara Thistle is mine."

Kara offered a low, throaty laugh. "You know, in the past I might've shot someone who said something like that. But the truth is—" she wrapped her arms around him "—I like the idea of being yours. I just wish it hadn't taken me so long to figure it out."

"Amen to that," he joked. "I thought I was going to have to throw you over my shoulder and hogtie you to the bed until you came to your senses."

Kara's gaze narrowed. "I definitely would've shot you for that."

Matthew threw his head back for a good laugh. "Well, it's a good thing I didn't try it." He sobered then, but his eyes retained the warmth of laughter as he added, "But I think it would've been worth it just to see the look on your face."

"You're a man who lives dangerously. Who knew you were such an adrenaline junkie," she teased, and then leaned her head against his solid chest. She sighed and then, turning her head to the side, gazed out the window. The truth was, he could've done all those things and more.

He'd already taken her heart, and her body had willingly followed—it was just her head that had needed convincing. But those days were blissfully over.

"Are you up to taking a walk on the beach?" he asked. "Briana wants to look for sea glass and seashells for her school project."

"Yep. I can't imagine anything I'd like to do more," she said, starting to pull away to get ready. But Matthew pulled her back with a mischievous glint in his eye.

"You can't imagine *anything?*"

Kara bit back a coy grin but her cheeks flushed at the suggestion in his expression. "Well...now that you mention it...I do have a bit of a headache. Perhaps you could spare a moment to help me out?"

"Sweetheart, I can't imagine anything I'd like to do more. And that's the truth." He laughed and they retreated to the bedroom for a little...headache remedy—Beauchamp-style.

COMING NEXT MONTH

Available August 31, 2010

HARLEQUIN®

A Romance

FOR EVERY MOOD™

Spotlight on

── Heart & Home ──

Heartwarming romances
where love can happen
right when you least expect it.

See the next page to enjoy a sneak peek
from Harlequin Superromance®,
a Heart and Home series.

Enjoy a sneak peek at fan favorite Molly O'Keefe's
Harlequin Superromance miniseries,
THE NOTORIOUS O'NEILLS, *with*
TYLER O'NEILL'S REDEMPTION,
available September 2010
only from Harlequin Superromance.

Police chief Juliette Tremblant recognized the shape of the man strolling down the street—in as calm and leisurely fashion as if it were the middle of the day rather than midnight. She slowed her car, convinced her eyes were playing tricks on her. It had been a long time since Tyler O'Neill had been seen in this town.

As she pulled to a stop at the curb, he turned toward her, and her heart about stopped.

"What the hell are you doing here, Tyler?"

"Well, if it isn't Juliette Tremblant." He made his way over to her, then leaned down so he could look her in the eye. He was close enough to touch.

Juliette was not, repeat, *not* going to touch Tyler O'Neill. Not with her fingers. Not with a ten-foot pole. There would be no touching. Which was too bad, since it was the only way she was ever going to convince herself the man standing in front of her—as rumpled and heart-stoppingly handsome now as he'd been at sixteen—was real.

And not a figment of all her furious revenge dreams.

"What are you doing back in Bonne Terre?" she asked.

"The manor is sitting empty," Tyler said and shrugged, as though his arriving out of the blue after ten years was casual. "Seems like someone should be watching over the family home."

"You?" She laughed at the very notion of him being here for any unselfish reason. "Please."

HSREXP0910

He stared at her for a second, then smiled. Her heart fluttered against her chest—a small mechanical bird powered by that smile.

"You're right." But that cryptic comment was all he offered.

Juliette bit her lip against the other questions.

Why did you go?

Why didn't you write? Call?

What did I do?

But what would be the point? Ten years of silence were all the answer she really needed.

She had sworn off feeling anything for this man long ago. Yet one look at him and all the old hurt and rage resurfaced as though they'd been waiting for the chance. That made her mad.

She put the car in gear, determined not to waste another minute thinking about Tyler O'Neill. "Have a good night, Tyler," she said, liking all the cool "go screw yourself" she managed to fit into those words.

It seems Juliette has an old score to settle with Tyler.
Pick up TYLER O'NEILL'S REDEMPTION
to see how he makes it up to her.
Available September 2010,
only from Harlequin Superromance.

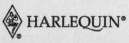

TANYA MICHAELS
Texas Baby

Instant parenthood is turning Addie Caine's life upside down. Caring for her young nephew and infant niece is rewarding—but exhausting! So when a gorgeous man named Giff Baker starts a short-term assignment at her office, Addie knows there's no time for romance. Yet Giff seems to be in hot pursuit.... Is this part of his job, or can he really be falling for her? And her chaotic, ready-made family!

**Available September 2010
wherever books are sold.**

"LOVE, HOME & HAPPINESS"

www.eHarlequin.com

HAR75325

MARGARET WAY

introduces

THE *Rylance* DYNASTY

The lives & loves of Australia's most powerful family

Growing up in the spotlight hasn't been easy, but the two Rylance heirs, Corin and his sister, Zara, have come of age and are ready to claim their inheritance. Though they are privileged, proud and powerful, they are about to discover that there are some things money can't buy....

Look for:

Australia's Most Eligible Bachelor

Available September

Cattle Baron Needs a Bride

Available October

www.eHarlequin.com

HRI7679

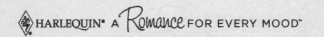